QUEEN TAKES KNIGHTS

THEIR VAMPIRE QUEEN, BOOK 1

JOELY SUE BURKHART

QUEEN TAKES KNIGHTS
THEIR VIRGIN QUEEN, book 1

Published by
Joely Sue Burkhart

**A lost virgin vampire queen. Two vampire knights
sworn to protect her.
It's about to get very hot... and bloody...**

Ever since her mother was murdered by monsters five years ago, Shara Isador has been on the run. Alone, scared, and exhausted, she's finally cornered in Eureka Springs, Arkansas. Out of hope with nowhere else to turn, she's ready to end it all when two men come to her rescue.

They say she's a lost queen descended from Isis, and they're her Blood, vampire knights sworn to protect her. It all seems like a crazy nightmare, until the alpha offers his blood. Then she realizes she's never wanted anything more. Except maybe his body... and his friend's, too.

But they're not the only ones searching for a lost queen. Shara must learn how to wield her new powers quickly and conquer her fears if she intends to keep them all alive.

For my Beloved Sis.
A special thank you to Sherri Meyer for beta reading.

1

SHARA

It sucked to be twenty two years old and still afraid of the dark.

Bad things always happened in the dark. I'd learned that at an early age, when my father was brutally murdered in front of me. My mother met the same fate when I was seventeen.

Waiting for the sun to set, monsters were real and they were always hungry. Always hunting.

Demons with pasty gray skin, wasted bodies down to skin and bones, with red, glowing eyes. Mom always said they were hunting her, but after she died, I kept seeing them.

They were still hunting... me.

I'd lose them for a few weeks at a time, but then I'd start to get that old familiar itch down my spine. I'd feel the eyes at dusk. Shadows crowded around my cheap room, testing the doors and windows, looking for a weak spot in paper-thin walls. It was always the same story, and at dawn, I'd head out to the bus stop and try to lose them again for a few days.

It didn't matter how careful I was. They always found me again, because they hunted by the smell of my blood. Thanks to my very regular menstrual cycle, I could count on them always finding me in under a month. And if I cut my finger, I'd better leave on the next bus as quickly as possible, knowing the scent was like a beacon shining over my location.

I'd been in Eureka Springs, Arkansas for about two weeks. Only a week until Christmas, but I'd be gone by then. The thought made me sad, because I actually liked this town. It had a deep, resonant feeling, like a ringing bell that I could almost hear. Maybe it was all the caves, natural springs, and deep cliffs that funneled its inhabitants' energy into a river I could almost touch.

I had a modest inheritance from my parents, but it wouldn't last forever, so I always tried to find a temporary job to cover my expenses. If I was extremely lucky, I could find a job cleaning motel rooms that let me have a cheap room for free. Eureka Springs had lots of small ma-and-pop type motels for the wedding business, but with the holidays, pickings were light. Most motels had already closed for the season, and my boss said it'd be a ghost town after the Christmas shopping died down.

I only knew the owner as Hosea. He'd been pretty nice to me so far, even letting me eat meals out of the small kitchen (as long as I was willing to help out waitressing tables or delivering food to the cabins) so I didn't have the heart to tell him I probably wouldn't make it that long.

"Yo, Shara," Hosea called, waving me toward the office. I started to tuck the cleaning cart into the storage closet, but he hollered, "No, bring it."

My nerves were already starting to jangle a warning. It was almost five in the evening. This time of year, it'd be full-on dark pretty quickly. I'd feel a lot better once I was safely in my room for the night.

I dragged the cart over and he smiled apologetically. His bald head gleamed in the light, his face lined and worn. He had the nicest eyes, though. So kind and good-hearted. Almost like my father's, from what I remembered. I hadn't met too many people with nice eyes over the years. "I know it's late, but we had an urgent clean-up call from the honeymoon cabin."

I'd made it clear I'd do just about anything he asked as far as cleaning the rooms or working in the kitchen—as long as I stayed indoors after nightfall.

The main motel was a lodge building, with rooms off one main hall. Over the years, he'd added individual cabins spaced out on the property, away from the main building. The customers loved being able to have a room "out in the woods" where they couldn't see anybody else, but still be minutes away from a hot meal or the main shopping strip.

The honeymoon cabin was bigger than the others with a giant heart-shaped Jacuzzi that I'd come to despise, and of course, it was the furthest from the main building. "The tub again?"

He nodded. "They put some bubbles in and lost track of how full it was getting."

Crap. I so did not want to track out there and mop for an hour or two.

"Ellie's home sick and Tom's in the kitchen. I really need you to take it if at all possible. I'll give you a bonus."

I could use the money, but my hands were already trembling. It was early. My period probably wouldn't start for another day or two, so the monsters shouldn't have tracked me this far. But that didn't mean they weren't out there, waiting for me to be stupid enough to walk around at night.

With a small nod, I turned around and headed down the hall to the back door. I'd stay inside as long as possible, take the shortest route there, and get back. I'd leave the cart and run if I had to. Pausing at the door, I crouched down and checked the bucket on the very bottom with my personal supplies. It wasn't much, just a large container of salt and a strip of wood with a few rusty old nails I'd scrounged. Salt and iron were about the only thing I'd found to deter the monsters long enough for me to get to safety. If I could make one of them bleed, the rest of the pack would usually attack the wounded one, buying me more time.

I didn't have much of a coat, just a pullover hoodie I now dragged over my head. The cold didn't bother me much, but I got a lot of weird stares if I walked around in the middle of winter without at least some long sleeves on. I checked my pocket, making sure the small pocketknife hadn't fallen out.

Taking a deep breath, I closed my eyes and tried to sense anything amiss. Was the trickle of ice down my spine my imagination brought about by fear? Or was there really something out there? I couldn't tell, but it might be the faint white line of salt I'd spilled at the door when I first came here. So far, no one had noticed and swept it up. It helped that they put salt on the sidewalks to keep them from being slippery. Another thing that might keep me somewhat safe tonight if I stuck to the sidewalk.

I stepped outside, my shoulders tight, my eyes straight ahead, and I walked with a mission. Five minutes, and I'd be at the cabin. Ten at most. My heart thudded with anxiety, but the air smelled incredible. Clean and fresh, frosty with a hint of snow. Pine trees thickened around the sidewalk, providing coverage from the city lights. A light dusting of snow crunched under my feet. For a moment, I was away from the noise of the streets, surrounded by nature's peace, and I relaxed despite my fears. I loved this place. It felt so… right. Natural. Maybe I could come back in a few months. I bet Hosea would take me on again, if he got as busy as he said in May and June.

The honeymoon cabin was constructed from logs of Arkansas pine and built up off the ground like a treehouse. It was actually really cool, though a lot of customers couldn't do the stairs. Hosea hoped to build a couple of more next summer that were more accessible. Grabbing the mop and bucket out of the cart, I climbed the double flight of stairs and paused a moment to scan the surrounding woods. Opening my senses, I tried to find anything out of place.

I imagined the area around me like a soft, billowing fabric.

Three dimensional trees, plants, and animals dotted the fabric, but they felt right. Natural. People were like blinking fireflies, floating here and there, or streaming in rivers that I knew were the highways downtown. Some areas glowed brighter, where more people gathered for dinner or work. The monsters always felt like a stain or small tear in that fabric. Nothing I could see with my eyes until it was too late, just a feeling of wrongness. But they were very good at hiding. Almost as good as me.

Something drew my attention to the south. Two warm spots glowed like tiny campfires, definitely red against the soft white fireflies of the people living around me. I'd never seen anything like that before. Monsters weren't warm and they didn't glow like this. The more I focused on those campfires, they hotter they burned. Molten fire, lava, thick and hot, bubbling up out of the earth. The glowing rivers of embers seemed to call me. I reached out slowly, listening, feeling, for anything bad. The red bubbled up higher, like it was seeking me too. So beautiful. I strained harder...

I about jumped out of my skin when someone touched me.

"Sorry," the man said. "Come in, it's freezing out here."

I looked back out over the forest, but the glowing red had only been in my mind. Sighing, I stepped into the one-room cabin. A small seating area looked cozy before a massive stone fireplace. A large king-sized four-poster bed dominated the rest of the room, with the hated Jacuzzi in the corner. Bubbles frothed over the top and onto the tiled floors. At least Hosea hadn't put wood floors in. They'd have been trashed a dozen times just since I'd been here. The bride sat on the edge of the bed wrapped in a towel, avoiding my gaze. Candles lined the tub, along with a half-drank bottle of wine and... ew. A used condom.

You wouldn't believe the disgusting crap housecleaning had to take care of.

I set to work, mopping, squeezing out the water, dumping the bucket outside, over and over until the mess was sopped up.

I changed out the soggy towels they'd thrown on the floor to sop up the first spills, and took the rug outside to hang on the deck railing. I'd be back out tomorrow and pick it up for a cleaning. The happy couple had finished the bottle of bubbly and popped open another while I slaved to clean up after them. At least they bothered to say, "thanks," as I headed back outside. No tip. Hopefully Hosea followed through with that promise of a bonus.

I checked my watch. One hour. A record cleaning, that was for sure, but it was pitch black outside. I threw my tools into the cart and started off on a rapid pace for the main building, scanning the woods around me.

The hair on the back of my neck prickled. I sensed a darkness, a nameless heaviness. Watching. To my left, up in the woods, high on a hill. But it saw me. It knew me. And I knew it. Him.

It was the same darkness who'd killed my mother.

I BROKE INTO A RUN, dragging the cart along the sidewalk. The tires skidded on the ice and the cart tried to overturn. I'd never make it back to safety with it.

Breathing hard, I stopped beneath the closest light pole and grabbed my small bucket of weapons. Using the meager shelter of the cart, I scanned the woods, using both my eyes and my sense of fabric of the area. There was a definite shadow creeping through the woods, and the watcher high up, though he hadn't come closer. The nightmare of my mother's murder tried to crowd into my brain. Gray shapeless monsters grabbing her. Dragging her. The tall dark shadow engulfing her. Blood spraying from her throat.

I shuddered and pushed the image away. Not now. I refused to panic. Panic would make me do something stupid. I'd escaped many times before. I'd escape again.

He won't have me tonight.

I started to stand, but caught another whiff of wrongness on the air, warning they were close. They were between me and the main cabin. They'd already cut me off.

Fuck.

I could probably make it back to the honeymoon cabin, but I didn't think the newlyweds would welcome my presence for long, if they even allowed me back inside. There'd be questions. I knew from experience that people always thought I was nuts if I started talking about monsters, and if I wasn't careful, I'd find myself sedated and committed. Easy pickings for the monsters. If I blabbed about monsters no one else could see, Hosea would would probably fire me. I couldn't afford any marks against my name for fear news would spread, and then I'd never get another job.

Shivering, but not with cold, I gathered my resolve. I was going to have to fight. So be it.

I stepped out a circle, trailing a thick line of salt on the ground, about six feet in diameter. Close enough I could defend it—but large enough that they wouldn't be able to touch me easily. I loaded my nailed club in my left hand, and the pocket knife in my right. Then I crouched down beside the cart and waited.

I felt the wrongness first. Like a discordant note that I couldn't quite hear, a flicker of shadow out of the corner of my eye, but when I looked, nothing was there. The smell intensified that sense of wrongness until I wanted to gag. Dead, rotting flesh, rolled in shit, and left in a putrid swamp to mold. It'd be even worse if I managed to injure one of them. *When*, I corrected myself sternly. Because if I didn't manage to create a diversion, I'd probably be torn apart long before dawn.

Only one monster crept toward my circle. They didn't like the light. Terror made me snicker out loud as I thought about them drawing straws to see which one had to try and get me first. Long, stringy hair hung down to its shoulders, but I couldn't tell from its shape if it had been a man or a woman. Its arms were twice as long as normal, creepy long bony fingers reaching out along the ground like a foul spider. It touched the salt and hissed.

But it kept touching the salt, digging scaly fingers through the grains, even as it started to howl, a terrible high-pitched screech that didn't sound like any living creature. Smoke broke from its darkened skin, yet it still tried desperately to break my circle.

I leaped forward and slammed the nailed club onto its forearm, then jerked back, making sure to tear the dead, hanging skin open.

From the shadows, a chittering sound rose up all around me. I shuddered, trying to keep my instincts in check. Even muscle in my body vibrated with alarm. They'd surrounded me. I had no option. I had to flee. Now.

Even though my brain knew I had no hope of escape. They wanted me to break into mindless terror and run. They'd love a good hunt through the woods.

The pack came closer, creeping out of the shadows, lured by the smell of blood. Even black, putrid blood. The injured one hissed at its friends as they closed on it, gnashing inch-long razor teeth, shredding its own lips, as if it was driven mad by blood hunger too. Even its own.

A sound behind me sent me whirling. I slammed the club down, trying to catch the other monster scratching through the salt. Missed.

Another screeched to my right. I slashed without looking and felt the drag of the knife blade through flesh.

They closed in. Ten. I'd never faced so many before.

I couldn't breathe with the stench. The terror. Their eyes glowed, the terrible clicking sound they made with their teeth sending goosebumps down my arms. I made a slow turn inside the circle, trying to think of a way to escape. A way to trick them. The one I'd wounded suddenly disappeared beneath two or three of the monsters, but the rest closed ranks around me.

It was almost like they'd learned from their previous attempts. Or maybe the watcher had managed to train them better. Either option spelled my death.

I thought again of my mother. How hard she'd tried to protect us. Rather than moving over and over like me, she'd built a fortress in an old stone mansion in Kansas City, Missouri. The walls were thick and stout, resisting even their attempts to burn us out once. We had a safe room deep below the house in the old cellars, lined in brick and stone, mortared with salt. We'd retreated to that room anytime the monsters gathered outside, and they hadn't been able to penetrate our safe room.

Until one managed to outsmart Mom by using a young kid as bait. They'd guessed correctly that she'd have a weakness for a child. That she'd never turn her back on a child in need.

That kindness had earned her death.

Me, I'd die because I didn't want to lose my lousy job cleaning up used condoms and bathtub floods.

I'd wanted so badly to run outside and help her, but she'd locked me in. She'd known I'd come after her if something bad happened. I hadn't been able to see much through the tiny window, other than the tall one tearing her throat open. I hoped she'd died quickly, but I had a feeling I would not be so lucky. Not after running from them for so long.

They're not going to torture me.

I straightened, standing to my full height. I saluted the dark watcher on the hill with the knife.

And then I lifted the blade to my own throat.

"Stop!" Someone bellowed, a deep male voice that hammered through the night like a bass drum. The monsters quailed, not quite turning tail to run, but definitely wary. "Wait, my queen! We're here!"

2

SHARA

Queen? What the actual fuck? I had no idea what the man meant. Who they were. Or why they were here. They, plural. Two men crashed through the trees, headed straight for me.

But they were definitely the distraction I needed.

I slashed to the left and right, wounding as many of the monsters as possible as they turned to attack the approaching men. I scanned my salt circle, relieved to see that it was still whole. I had no idea who these guys were, or how they thought they could fight the monsters, when no one else had ever even seen them, let alone actually tried to help me.

For all I knew, these two were in league with the watcher. I wasn't going to step out of the little bit of safety I had on a *maybe* they were going to help.

They both had unusual blades, that compared to my pock-etknife, were almost as big as swords. The sharp blades fit over their hands somehow, becoming an extension of their arms. The blades chopped through heads and limbs effortlessly. I'd never been able to kill one of the monsters, let alone so many. Yet the monsters weren't giving up so easily. One launched itself onto the taller man's back, digging claws into his flanks. The other man grabbed a handful of lanky hair, hauled the monster's head back, and sawed through its throat. Black blood stained them both, but it was the fresh blood pouring from the taller man's side that caught my attention.

I'd seen blood before. No big deal. It didn't gross me out, but it'd never fascinated me, either.

But his blood...

I couldn't look away.

I don't know if it was my imagination, shock and adrenaline from the battle, but his blood glowed like rubies in the streetlight, bubbling up from his side like the molten lava I'd seen earlier. Two spots of red on the fabric I'd never seen before, and now two men here, helping me.

When I'd never had help in my entire life.

The remaining monsters—only three still living—scattered. Leaving the two men turning their attention to me.

Panting, the tall, wounded man neared the edge of my circle but didn't step across it. Maybe he couldn't? I didn't know. I didn't care. I couldn't look away from his blood. My mouth actually watered, which made my stomach knot. What the hell was wrong with me?

"Do you have a safe place nearby?"

I dragged my gaze away from the blood seeping through his shredded T-shirt and made myself focus on his eyes. Normal eyes as far as I could tell. They didn't glow red like the monsters. "Who are you?"

"Alrik and Daire. We're yours, my queen. If you'll have us."

"Why do you keep calling me a queen?"

The two men looked at each other, some silent communication I didn't understand. Then the tall one looked back at me again. "We will explain everything, once you're safe. A master thrall still watches to the east. I'd rather get you into shelter before we answer any questions you will have."

Yes, I still felt the watcher, thrall, he'd called it. They had information, which I desperately needed. And they'd helped. Yet I remembered how my mother had been lured to her death. Betrayed by her own desire to protect a little kid.

These weren't children, but full-grown, very large men, now that they both stood so closely. Alrik, the bigger one, was arguably the most massive person I'd ever seen short of a super-hero movie. The other was shorter and leaner. Both had longer shoulder-length hair and those double hand knives, but they dressed like normal everyday people in jeans, T-shirts, and boots.

T-shirts. Not long sleeves. The cold didn't bother them either.

Still doubtful, I watched them remove the blades from their hands, snapping them to hooks on their belt on either hip. It almost looked like Old West gun holsters. "Can you not cross the circle?"

Holding my gaze, Alrik took another step closer, ignoring the salt that had kept the monsters out. That put him close enough to touch. "I only thought to be polite."

I don't know why I did it. I've never been comfortable touching people. I don't hug. I've never had sex. Never felt any kind of attraction to anyone to even try. But I reached out and dragged my index finger through the blood on his side. Even though I had an open knife in my hand, he didn't back away.

His blood was hot, tingling on my skin. The insane urge to step closer and press my mouth to that wound came over me and I shuddered, involuntarily taking a step back.

But he snagged my elbow, gently tugging me back to him.

"Take what you want from me, my queen."

I SHOULD HAVE JABBED the pocketknife up into his ribs, but the simple touch of his fingers on my elbow stalled my brain. It was like my entire system overloaded in a flash and broke down.

Shock, I told myself, but I wasn't cold or shivering or sweating or even scared. Not any longer. He cupped the back of my head, his fingers tangling in my hair, and my fight or flight instincts still didn't kick in. That, more than anything, scared me. I'd always been able to count on my instincts to keep me alive.

"If you feed her for the first time here, you might not be able to stop." The other man spoke for the first time, and I could hear the amusement in his voice.

I pulled back, and Alrik let me go, though he did make a low sound that almost sounded like a groan. Surely a huge tough guy like him wouldn't make a sound like that.

I glanced at the other man and the smirk on his face told me I hadn't been mistaken.

"Who are you again?" My voice rang with confusion, accusation, a thousand questions I didn't even know how to voice.

"Alrik and Daire," the one with the smirk said. "Your Blood, if you'll take us. You can think of us as... knights. Though we don't wear shining armor."

Slightly different wording, take versus have. The way he said it, he'd meant it as a playful dare. So his name fit his personality perfectly. He stepped closer, ignoring my line of salt too. His fingers closed around my makeshift nail club and gently took it from me. He examined it in the light and whistled softly.

"Crude, but effective. Well done, my queen."

My knife was next. He arched a brow at me, as if to say surely I could do better, but then he wiped it clean on his pants and offered the closed pocketknife back to me.

As I slipped it back into my pocket, I had to admit, I wanted a pair of those hand blades he used, though I wasn't sure how I'd get through security with those in my pack. "Why do you call me that? I have no idea what's going on here."

"Give us your name and we'll call you that instead of queen, if you like."

I couldn't see any harm in giving these strangers my name. They had helped me, after all. "Shara."

"And your family?"

They both stared at me intently, a strange urgency growing in their eyes. Why would they need to know my last name? "My father's name—"

"No," Alrik broke in. "Your mother's."

"Selena." I didn't immediately offer her last name. Mom had told me it was a secret. That it wasn't safe. I should always use Dad's surname, Dalton, even though she hadn't married him. Her surname was her last gift to me. I didn't know how, I just knew, now, that my life depended on giving them that same gift. "Isador."

If anything, their intensity ratcheted up another notch, though I had no idea why. I hated not knowing what was going on. Why my name might be important, or why these two strangers might recognize my mother's name.

The one with the smirk pressed the pad of his thumb to one of the rusty old nails on my club. His blood welled, and as before, I found myself unable to look away. He slowly lifted his bleeding thumb toward my face, giving me every opportunity to flinch away. Flee. Stab him with my knife. But I stood there, shaking, fighting my own urge.

I wanted to launch myself against the big one and lick his wound. And then turn and suck the blood from his friend's thumb.

What the hell is wrong with me?

Daire smoothed his bleeding thumb across my bottom lip.

Fire exploded on me. At least that's what it felt like. Flames licking my skin, a poisonous, addictive drug suddenly hitting my veins when I reflexively licked my lips. My eyelids fluttered. My pulse pounded in my skull so hard I thought it might shatter. My knees quivered. One big arm slid around my back, catching me, pulling me up against a sheer wall of muscle.

14

My body jolted against his, shocked at the contact. And Daire took the opportunity to slide his thumb into my mouth.

His blood, hot on my tongue. My jaws clamped down on him, trapping his thumb in my teeth, but he didn't complain. He only made a low, rumbly sound of pleasure.

"So you can feed her, but I can't, dickhead?"

"Sorry." Daire didn't sound apologetic though.

This couldn't be happening. I wasn't in one stranger's arms, sucking his friend's thumb to get more blood from the tiny wound. But I made a noise that sounded suspiciously like frustration, because no more blood oozed from his thumb.

"Use your fangs, Shara."

My name on his lips did insane things to my body. It sounded so... filthy, coming from him. Like he was thinking of something else I should be sucking instead of his thumb.

And fangs. What the fuck? Again, I had no idea what he meant.

I smelled something delicious close by, though. So I released his thumb and turned my face toward the man holding me. I touched my lips to his bloody shirt and the big man trembled. His hands tightened reflexively and his chest rumbled on a deep growl. Unsure, I started to pull back, but he clamped my head to him and swept me up in his arms.

"Safety," Alrik ground out. "Or I'm carrying you to my bike and driving till dawn."

His blood coated my lips, stirring a heat in me that I've never felt before. It felt...sexual. His big body against me, hard muscle working as I took his blood. And I wanted more. I wanted it all. His body and his blood.

For the first time in my life, I realized that I wasn't exactly human.

Fangs. Blood. My body had made the connection, even if my brain still stuttered around helplessly, refusing to believe the evidence.

Maybe I should have been alarmed. Maybe I should have

adamantly denied any such urges. But honestly, it was a fucking relief.

I'd always been different, and so damned alone once I lost Mom. If these two men were like me, I was sticking close. Until they gave me a reason not to.

3

SHARA

Their blood tasted better than anything I'd ever had in my life and it went straight to my head like a suicide-shot of caffeine, adrenaline, wine, and chocolate, mixed with a cocaine chaser. I didn't want to stop tasting him. I didn't think I'd ever get enough.

Alrik cupped my cheek, pulling my face up toward his. I struggled a moment, but only because I wanted more. Then I remembered the danger we were in, and the watcher on the hill. He was still there, and I could feel his rage creeping through the woods like a foul poison.

I tipped my head toward the lodge. "I have a room in the motel. It's kept me safe for two weeks."

He looked at his friend and I had a sense of words unspoken flowing between them. Then Daire turned to leave and sudden panic gripped me. I reached out and caught a handful of his shirt. "Where are you going?"

Turning to me, he pressed his forehead to mine, wrapping me and his friend in his arms. "Never fear that I'll leave you. I'd sooner die first. I'm going to grab our wheels and bring them up to your location so we can leave at dawn."

17

"But how will you find my room?"

"Rik will tell me. We've shared blood many times and it creates a bond. I will find him. I'll stay close, but you may want some privacy."

Privacy. That word carried so many layers and implications. I became aware of two male bodies pressed against me, and the very hard evidence of their desire. Both of them.

More, I became aware of my own.

Need pulsed through me, fed by their blood. I ached in places that had never stirred with desire before. I wanted their hands, their mouths, and their cocks. I trembled between them, imagining it. Wrapped in their heat, taking their blood, taking their bodies. Nothing had ever sounded better to me in my entire life. I didn't want *only* Alrik. Or only Daire.

I wanted this. Both of them. Holding me all night long.

I'd been without any kind of physical contact for so long, not a handshake or a hug, let alone pure physical desire. I'd never felt like this, and I wasn't ready to let it go. They might be willing to share and take turns, but I wasn't.

"No," I said hoarsely. "No privacy. I want you. I want him. And I don't want either of you out of my sight."

"Greedy," Daire teased, kissing my nose. "I like it. I'll be fast."

He didn't release me, though, only staring at me with an expectant look in his eyes. They called me queen. Maybe he truly wanted my permission. I gave him a nod and he let go of me, turned, and... blurred. That quickly, he was gone.

"What are you?" I whispered. He didn't even leave tracks in the snow.

What am I?

Something inside me whispered back. *You know. You've always known.*

Alrik cradled me in his arms and took a step. That's what it felt like. A single step. And we stood outside the motel. He opened the door and strode down the hall. I worried about

Hosea seeing me carried off by some big man, but Alrik did the same blurring thing. One step, and we were past the desk, outside my door.

"Here?"

I nodded and he set me down while I dug in my pockets and found the key card. The door beeped and I started forward, but he wrapped his palm around my throat, his grip gentle but firm as he drew me back against him. Shielding me with his body, he carefully eased his way into the room, as if he feared an invasion while we were gone.

His strength felt nice, I had to admit. I'd been alone and struggling for so long, terrified the monsters would find me while I slept, or tracked me down in between jobs. Having a powerful man to fight the monsters off would be a relief. That I was also attracted to him, only made it all the sweeter. And he didn't intimidate me. He wasn't squeezing my throat, threatening me harm. It was like he just wanted to touch me. A vulnerable place for sure, and intimate, without being vulgar.

I flipped on the light and he took a slow look about the room. His body tensed against me and I started to worry maybe he was right. Maybe one of the monsters had managed to break through the salt line and my locked door. I'd asked for no windows, but maybe one had found its way through the vent. Or...

He turned to me, his mouth a hard slant and his eyes glittering with what I could only call rage.

"I find it intolerable that the vampire queen of Isador has been living in such squalor."

4

ALRIK

escended from Isis herself, Shara Isador stood before me, completely unaware of her heritage. Her power. Her legacy.

How was that possible?

I knew, but I hated it. I hated that I hadn't been able to find her for all these years. That I hadn't been serving at her side.

The last Isador queen, the royal line lost for over thirty years. The shit would definitely hit the proverbial fan when the Triune heard.

Shara. Her name resonated in me, etched in my bones. As soon as I'd felt the slight touch of her mind searching in the darkness, I'd been hers. I couldn't get to her fast enough.

She shrugged. "This is actually one of the better places I've stayed. It's clean, safe, and Hosea, my boss, even lets me eat for free."

The thought of my queen hungry, scared, and alone made me quiver with rage.

"Vampires." She laughed, shaking her head. "Not something I would have ever guessed. The monsters hunting me?

Sure. But not me. I'd say you must be joking, but…" She averted her gaze, her cheeks flushing. "I've never tasted anything as good as your blood before."

I concentrated on keeping my anger contained. It wasn't her fault that her mother had left her legacy behind and died, alone, without any Blood to protect her. Though how Selena could have thought to stay alive for long exiled from her own kind, I had no idea. Evidently she hadn't taught her daughter much about our way of life, either. "The monsters are thralls, once human. The watcher on the hill is their master, once one of our kind. They were his human victims when he lost his queen."

She shivered, her eyes widening. "Then we could become monsters like that?"

"You? No. Never. Queens are only ever queens."

"All women our kind are queens?"

I could not believe this. She knew nothing, absolutely nothing, about her legacy. It was unconscionable. "No. Not at all. A queen is a rare and precious thing."

I felt Daire's nearness a moment before he tapped and opened the door. He recoiled at the living conditions our queen had endured and shot me a dark look.

:What the ever loving fuck?:

:It's worse. She knows nothing about her legacy. About us. Absolutely nothing.:

:Selena must have died before she could teach her.:

Aloud, I asked, "How old were you when your mother died?"

"Almost seventeen."

Daire shook his head. "Fucking shit."

She looked at him, her eyebrows rising. Drawing herself up, she looked every inch a queen. My heart swelled with pride, hope, desperate longing to formalize my service. What a queen we'd found. "You have something to say, say it."

Daire wasn't one to mince words. "If Selena wanted to

abandon her nest and free her Blood, fine. But as soon as she conceived you, she should have immediately sent you to the nearest queen. You should never have been alone, lost, abandoned like this. This…" he waved his arms around the room. "Makes me want to paint the streets with blood."

"Mom would never have sent me away or abandoned me. It's not her fault that she died."

"You're wrong. It *is* her fault. She should never have been alone."

Maybe she was still buzzed on the first taste of our blood, but I suspected our queen naturally had a fiery temper. She strode to Daire, eyes blazing, and poked him in the chest hard enough he grunted.

She was so beautiful that I hurt, deep inside, to look at her. Sleek, dark hair, large dark eyes, high cheekbones and forehead, long elegant legs, the figure of a goddess. So fucking regal.

"She wasn't alone. She had me."

"A child who knew nothing about her legacy. Now a grown woman, struggling to survive alone, hunted all her days, when she could have a dozen powerful Blood at her side to satisfy her every desire."

"A dozen?" She laughed, shaking her head. "I only see two."

"They will come," I whispered, torn between eagerness and dread. I was Daire's alpha. But would an alpha come to take my place at the head of her Blood? Likely. I was young yet (for our kind, only eighty eight) and had never served a queen before. A Blood's power came from his queen, so I had nothing to gauge my own strength against.

I wanted her well protected and powerful, and the more Blood she had, the better off we'd all be. She'd gain power from her Blood, and we would gain power from her. The more we fed from her, the more our power would cascade, ever higher. So I would relish this time as her alpha as long as possible.

"Seriously? A dozen?"

"Marne Ceresa had a hundred Blood in her prime, though now more sibs than true Blood."

Shara shook her head slowly. "I have no idea what you're talking about."

"Did your mother teach you nothing?"

I was glad Daire said it, though I was thinking it.

"About sibs and thralls and queens? No." She sat on the edge of the shabby bed. "She told me some stories about growing up in London, how she met Dad, that she left her family because they didn't approve."

As the alpha, I felt it my duty to break the darkness of the past to her. "Selena Isador had ten Blood when she took a human thrall. The ten were fine warriors, all dedicated to her service, but she loved the human. He didn't like the fact that she regularly fed and fucked her Blood. He didn't understand our ways. She was also taking heat from the Triune for bringing a human so deep into her nest. She finally decided to walk away. She dissolved the Blood and abandoned the Isador nest, leaving with only her human lover. Without the Blood, she had no protection, and her power diminished greatly over time. Eventually, even the Triune could not feel her presence any longer. She'd withered too much with none of our kind's blood to fuel her power. Then, she was gone. No one knew she had a child until you gave us your name."

Shara gnawed on her lip, her eyes swimming with tears. "She always said she loved Dad too much. When he died, I think she lost part of herself. She was never the same."

I squatted down before her, unable to bear her sadness without offering comfort. I took her hand in both of mine, and she leaned forward, hesitantly, as if unsure her touch would be welcome.

I wanted to haul her into my arms and rail curses on her mother for what she had done, but I only tipped my head down to hers, as Daire had done earlier. Submission, acceptance, my silent oath to serve in any way possible.

23

"I want to know everything."

Daire knelt beside me and I didn't have to look at him to know he was flashing a cocky smile. "Would you honestly rather have a history lesson now, when you could be fucking us both?"

5

DAIRE

According to legend, a queen's gifts naturally drew the Blood to her who were best suited for her strengths, needs and personality. I would always be the one to break the ice, make her laugh, or flirt and even antagonize her into furious, glorious fucking. Which both Rik and I desperately wanted.

She turned those gleaming eyes on me and I shuddered beneath her gaze. For a lost queen with no understanding of her legacy, she bore great power already. How great would she be when well fed on our blood?

There were many ways a Blood signaled submission to his queen. Kneeling before her like this, was one. Offering his throat, another.

Leaning closer to her, offering myself up, I tipped my head to the side and bared my throat.

She struck hard, her teeth gripping the column of my neck. I squeezed my thighs, keeping my hands off her until she had taken what she wanted. She gnawed on my skin and it hurt, yeah. But I fucking loved it. She couldn't ever hurt me enough to satisfy me. Even Rik, with all his size and strength, had never hurt me beyond my limit.

She made a low, desperate sound of frustration and I couldn't help but cup her face. "I can't do it. I don't know how. And I don't want to hurt you."

"You could never hurt me, my queen. Since you're half human, it's possible that you don't have fangs. I don't think we've ever had a half-human queen before."

She looked at me with such a look of desperation that I lifted my wrist to my mouth and shredded the skin for her. I offered my bleeding wrist and she grabbed me like a toddler tackling her first birthday cake. Closing my eyes, I sank against her. Her mouth on my skin. Her power rising. Hairs rose on my arms, my spine tingling, bones melting. Something rose inside me, a dark, hungry beast I carried, waiting to be brought out into the world. Rising to my queen's call. My skin rippled, bones aching and cracking under the force of power. I groaned, eager to embrace the gift. I'd waited my whole life for this. But the beast prowled back down inside me, still locked.

It needed a queen's blood to be completely free.

She lifted her mouth and looked at me, her eyes going wide with realization of what she'd done. Blood smeared her face, trickling down my fingers, splattering on the floor and the bed and her jeans.

I'd never seen anything more perfect in my life than my blood smeared on her lush lips.

"Did I take too much?"

I snorted, pressing closer to her. "Even starved all your life, you couldn't drink enough to harm me. Your stomach simply isn't big enough to hold that much."

She looked at the raw wound on my wrist, still dripping blood. "Shouldn't you close that? Bind it? Something?"

"Why? It's only blood."

"They hunt by blood," she whispered, shivering.

"They hunt *your* blood," Rik said, his voice deep and

booming so much she jumped against me. She didn't know him well enough yet to understand he wasn't angry or even jealous— just aroused to the point of pain, aching to give her his blood and his body. Rik was too fucking eager to feel his power rise at her touch, and desperate for his first taste of royal blood. Same as me. "Our blood is a warning to their kind. We're here, we're close, and we're willing to die to keep you safe. When you establish a permanent nest, we'll fucking bleed on every inch of it, though it's your blood that will give the nest its power."

We'd been sibs to the New York City Queen, Keisha Skye, for awhile, but never served her directly. We were not to her taste, since she preferred women, though her Blood and sibs had used us occasionally. It wasn't a fulfilling life.

Not for Aima in our prime, dreaming of serving our own queen.

Luckily, we'd been allowed to leave in search of weaker queens that Keisha could pull to her support. Rik had a crazy idea to follow thralls in the hope that one would lead us to a queen who didn't have many Blood, and so we'd left the cities and roamed together. Feeding each other, sibs only to ourselves. I loved the shit out of Rik and would die for him, but we both burned for a queen. We burned to be Blood, those who bleed in her service. After years of roaming from one coast of America to the other with no luck, we'd given up hope.

Until the faintest touch in the most unlikely, unglamorous state of Arkansas drew us to Shara fucking Isador.

Beautiful. Untouched. Lost.

Isis's own daughter.

Fuck.

The power she was going to have once she took us both. Even the Triune might sit up and take notice at the upstart half-human American vampire queen.

SHARA

I COULDN'T BELIEVE IT. I was a fucking vampire.

And Daire's blood tasted... incredible. Like a thousand of the world's most expensive, rare wines all blended together, sprinkled with fine crystal and gold. Heat pumped through my veins, as if my body had already managed to turn his blood into energy. My senses sharpened. I could still smell the musk of his skin. I threaded my fingers through his tousled hair, marveling at the softness of the multi-colored strands. It reminded me of a dark lion's mane, streaked with threads of gold. He even smelled a bit like what I'd imagined a big cat would smell like. Wild and dangerous.

I'd honestly forgotten all about Alrik. Until he planted his hands on either side of my hips on the bed and leaned in, muscling the other man out of the way. For a moment, I thought Daire might object, or even start a fight, but he yielded without complaint. Though he did shoot a sultry wink at me as he scooted to the side.

"My turn." Alrik growled. "My queen."

He smelled different from Daire. More like sweat and hot iron and a hint of smoke.

Yum, on both accounts.

"Are you too injured?"

Daire made a choked noise of amusement, while Alrik frowned. Evidently, I'd insulted him gravely.

"It's an honor to bleed for you, Shara. A minor injury is nothing but an opportunity to serve."

"Let me see how bad it is."

His eyelids went heavy, and he readily dragged the torn, stained shirt over his head and tossed it over his shoulder.

Oh. My. Fucking. Hot. Man. Alert.

I'd known he was a massive man, but the shirt had hid exactly how cut and well-defined his muscles were.

I ran my hands over the broad, heavy muscles of his chest

and shoulders, reveling in his strength. He was so ripped I could feel the fiber of muscle and tendon beneath his skin. Heat radiated off him, his body one massive furnace of lust and strength.

I ran my fingers down the chiseled ridges of his abs and found the slash in his side. It'd stopped bleeding, so I didn't think it was too deep. "Does it need to be cleaned? Bandaged?"

"Not at all. Our blood pushes out any toxins from the thrall's teeth and claws, and we heal quickly when well fed. It should be healed by morning. It's truly nothing."

"It's not nothing to me," I whispered, looking back up into his eyes, letting him see my gratitude. "No one has ever helped me like that before. Let alone been hurt doing so. If you hadn't come tonight..."

He made a low, rumbling sound. A threat, I thought, because I'd been so close to ending my life in order to avoid being eaten alive.

"Never again, Shara. You will never be alone and unprotected again."

I leaned in and rubbed my face on his throat, breathing in his scent. "That sounds good to me. Especially if I can have this too."

"Always. Take my blood. Take my body. Use me any way you desire. I'm yours."

My mouth ached, but I ran my tongue over my teeth and didn't feel anything new. I'd enjoyed biting Daire, even though I couldn't break the skin easily. I'd liked having him in my mouth.

Alrik rubbed his thumb gently over my lips. "Let me show you where the fangs should be, and feel if anything is there."

I opened my mouth and he stroked his index finger around the inside behind my teeth. He passed over a spot on one side and my breath caught. Sensation shot through me, a bolt of nerve endings coming alive. I ran my tongue around the front of my teeth and pressed on the other side, giving myself another jolt.

"They're there, though not quite ready to erupt." His voice

29

oozed with satisfaction, as if he couldn't wait for me to pierce him with my teeth.

Truth be told, I couldn't wait either.

"Daire, why don't you show her how it's done this time?"

"Gladly," Daire purred as he draped over the big man's shoulder. He wrapped his palm around the front of Alrik's neck and stroked the side of his throat. "Feel the pulse here."

I leaned forward and pressed my lips to that spot, slightly open so I could touch my tongue to Alrik's skin. His pulse thumped hard and steady beneath my tongue. Teasing him, I closed my teeth on his neck, testing how hard I could bite before he reacted. My mouth throbbed in beat with his pulse. I imagined sinking teeth deep into him, feeling his blood rush into my mouth, and I groaned.

Which made him groan.

Daire laughed. "Allow me, my queen."

I leaned back enough to watch, but kept my palms on Alrik's chest. I couldn't stop running my hands over his skin. Daire touched him too, holding his throat, sliding an arm around his waist to draw him back against him. And it suddenly dawned on me.

They'd been feeding each other, in more ways than one.

Daire licked Alrik's throat, flattening his tongue in firm, long strokes that made Alrik's head fall back against his shoulder with a deep, shuddering groan. He might as well have been sucking his dick. When he bit Alrik, it was just as intimate as sliding into his ass. Alrik arched his back, thrusting against me.

And I could suddenly see exactly how it would be with them. One of them fucking the other, while one fucked me. Dripping blood all over each other.

I shuddered, pressing closer, and reached down to Alrik's crotch. I don't think you could exist in this century and not know the basics of sex, but I'd never actually seen a man's dick before. Thanks a lot, ridiculous sexist television that didn't hesitate to show a woman's genitals but never a man's.

My fingers itched to explore him. Trace the ridges and veins, see what made him gasp and shudder. I wasn't shy. Far from it. And now that I had the opportunity to play with him and his friend, I sure as hell was going to enjoy them as much as they could endure.

Daire lifted his mouth a moment, letting blood trail down Alrik's chest for me. I licked the trails up toward the punctures while I jerked his jeans open. I pushed my hand down into the front of his pants and wrapped my fingers around his cock. So hard, so thick, and yet incredibly soft. I squeezed my thighs around his hips, burning for his hands. His mouth. That delicious cock sinking deep into me.

Yet he didn't even touch me.

I moaned against his skin, but I didn't want to leave his blood long enough to ask him to touch me.

His blood burned down my throat, so good. It had a kick, an extra punch, that Daire's hadn't. It went straight to my head like a shot of whiskey and I squeezed Alrik's dick harder.

Locking my mouth over the punctures Daire had made for me, I drank Alrik down like a woman dying of thirst. Daire's hair trailed over my cheek and then I felt his tongue, licking at my mouth and Alrik's skin. I made room for him, tipping my head so I could look him in the eyes. While we both fed on Alrik, licking his skin, finding each other's mouths.

I licked Alrik's blood from Daire's lips, his tongue sliding into my mouth as we shared the blood, and that's what broke the big man's reserve.

Alrik wrapped his arms around me, clutching me hard against him.

"Which do you want first, my queen: dick or fangs?"

I drew him through my fist, watching the way his nostrils flared. "Both."

6

SHARA

I tugged the hoodie over my head, and Alrik quickly followed with my T-shirt. I stood so I could get my jeans off, which was maybe a mistake. Because Alrik pressed his mouth to my stomach, and Daire reached for my bra over his back.

"We must take precautions," Alrik said against my stomach.

I peeled the denim down my thighs, trying to figure out what he meant. "Like birth control? Condoms? I guess I thought vampires were excluded from that kind of thing."

Daire snorted. "We are. You'll decide if and when you want an heir. That's the least of our concerns."

I started to sit down to finish pulling my shoes and pants off, but Alrik untied my tennis shoes and I toed them off, holding on to his shoulders.

"Your power." Alrik glanced up at me, and I was surprised to see worry written in lines between his eyes. "When it comes, we'll feel it too, and we'll be coming into our power as well. We'll all be vulnerable for a while."

"Not to mention the fallout." Daire dipped down to kiss my

shoulder. "For all we know, you may bring the whole building down on top of us."

I curled my arm up, holding my bra over my breasts. I wouldn't say shyness came over me. Just a feeling of vulnerability. A hint of shock creeping in.

A little over an hour ago, I'd been cleaning a tub as quickly as possible because I was afraid of monsters hiding in the dark.

Now I'd fed on two men. We were vampires. And I was about to have sex for the first time.

I wanted them, no doubt or hesitation at all. In fact, I was relieved to finally feel desire. My body was ready to jump right in, but my mind wanted a moment to catch up.

"Is it sex that brings the power?"

"No." Alrik handled each of my feet gently, stripping off my socks and helping me step out of my jeans. "It's blood. That's where the power lies. Sex is just a bonus that makes it even better. Now that you've fed from us, your power will rise. The more blood you take, the greater the power. It might be tonight, or days from now, but it will come, and sometimes it's like a bomb going off. And when you feed us, our power will rise as well."

"Good sex flavors the blood and makes it all the more powerful," Daire added. "It's possible to share blood but not sex, or sex but not blood, but most of us can't resist the combination."

I didn't feel powerful. How could someone who'd been scared most of their life feel powerful? But it did make sense in a way. I knew the monsters hunted me because of my blood.

"You're Isis's daughter, so the power will be great," Daire said. "I hope there's no cemetery close by."

I searched his eyes, confused. "Why?"

"She was known for bringing people back from the dead."

Oh. Crap. "Really? Mom never said anything like that."

If she'd had that kind of power, why didn't she save Dad? She'd run from the house and down the street to help us, screaming like a mad woman. Dad had thrown me up on his shoulders, keeping me out of reach of the two monsters that had ambushed us. It wasn't dark yet, but the risky pink and lavender time of dusk. We'd lost track of time, playing softball in the park.

The monsters cut his legs and knees until he fell. They tried for me, but I was able to bash one in the skull with my bat. But the other one ripped out Dad's throat.

Mom had wailed like something from a horror movie. But without hesitation, she'd picked me up and raced for the house.

Leaving Dad bleeding on the street.

"Every queen's power is different, even in the same line, though similar," Alrik said. "The goddesses decide what gifts to give, but each line has its own unique…" He hesitated, either trying to find the right word, or afraid to say it.

"Flavor," Daire finished for him.

"True, but that wasn't quite the word I was searching for."

"Curse?"

Alrik grimaced. "I don't want to scare her."

I wanted to say that I didn't scare easily, but I knew that wasn't true. Not with those monsters running around the woods hunting me everywhere I went.

I shivered, tightening my arms over my front.

Several moments went by before I realized something very important.

Both men simply knelt there. Waiting.

They didn't touch me, even though they wanted me. I'd just had Alrik's dick in my fist. I'd had as much of their blood as I'd wanted, and I stood here, nearly naked, and they didn't press their advantage.

I met Alrik's gaze but didn't say anything. I didn't have to.

"You're our queen, Shara. Our life. Our blood is yours to command. If you want our blood and nothing else, that is how it will be."

"I don't want that," I whispered, letting my bra fall away. "I want it all. It's just... I've never done this before."

Alrik's eyes narrowed and he looked angry again, like when he'd seen my room. Which was damned near a palace compared to some of the dumps I stayed in. Then he looked at Daire, and this time, I heard his words in my head.

:Unfucking believable. A virgin queen at her age.:

:A travesty.: Daire winked at me. Evidently he knew I was eavesdropping.

"Um," I said aloud, not wanting to betray a confidence. "I can hear you."

"Of course," Alrik replied, each word short and bit off. "You've had our blood. You can access our thoughts now."

"Why are you angry?"

Even on his knees, he looked up at me and somehow managed to glare and look intimidating. "*My* queen does not suffer in silence with no one to ease her need. My queen is not alone. My queen is not hungry, sad, hurting, or scared. My queen will have as much pleasure as you can stand. And for that reason, I suggest you allow Daire to entertain you with his mouth. None's as good as he, and that will ensure the rest is just as enjoyable for you."

MY EYES MET Daire's and he leaned forward slightly, but didn't touch me.

Power. I was starting to understand what they meant, but this power had nothing to do with blood or magical vampire shit. I could stand here, topless, and Daire wouldn't touch me until I gave him permission. Even if he desperately wanted to do so.

Both men had let me take their blood and touch them as I wanted, intimately, in Alrik's case. Yet they had barely touched me at all.

I felt a surge of confidence, not just in myself, but in them, too. I might not know them well yet, but I could trust them implicitly. They proved that every moment that they waited for my permission.

It was like throwing back heavy drapes in a room that had been closed off from the sunlight for decades. I hadn't even realized how dark and gloomy my life had been. I'd gotten used to being alone, unable to trust anyone.

I tangled fingers in his hair and pulled his face against my chest. His lips touched my skin, dancing across the tops of my breasts in soft, light kisses. The rasp of his tongue on my nipple made me jolt in his arms. He looked up at me, checking my reaction. Or maybe he just wanted to watch the way my head rolled back when he took my breast into the heat of his mouth. His tongue curled and stroked over my nipple and I shivered as sensation poured through me. Nerves flared to life, a cascading pleasure circuit that coursed through my veins. He switched to my other breast and my knees quivered. He licked a path down my stomach with small, teasing nips on my flanks and hipbones.

He nudged his face against my crotch, a playful bump that still made me groan. His tongue stroked over the top of my panties and I suddenly couldn't get them off fast enough. As soon as I pushed them down my hips, he took over and pulled them down to my feet.

Alrik swept me up against him and took me down to my bed. Startling hot skin pressed against mine and I wanted to stretch out between them and just soak them in, front to back. My skin felt starved for contact, as if it'd withered and died for this, never knowing this was exactly what I needed so desperately.

I forced my eyes open and lifted my head enough to see Daire. I drank in the powerful lines of his body. He wasn't as bulky and ripped as Alrik, his muscles more sleek and lithe yet still promising danger and strength. He shucked his pants and then planted a knee on the mattress to join us. The bed frame creaked and he shot a worried look at Alrik. "This rickety bed might not hold us all."

Alrik brushed his mouth against mine, drawing my attention to him, even as Daire kissed my calf. "We must provide our queen with a better, hardier bed."

I tried to picture a dozen men like him all standing around, either watching or joining or… I had no idea, not really. But it made my mouth quirk against his. "Big enough for a dozen Blood?"

"Yes, if that's what you want."

Daire made a slow path up my legs, lingering on my knees, his fingers gliding up and down my calves, massaging my muscles. Rubbing the arches of my feet. Then back up above my knee, loosening my quadriceps. The strength in his hands made me melt with pleasure. Years of fighting, running, struggling to survive relaxed inch by inch as he made his way up my body.

"Let us take care of you," Alrik whispered against my mouth. His fingers trailed across my collarbone and down my arm, bringing my skin to life. "Let us love you."

I think he meant make love *to* you, not love you, but right now, luxuriating in their gentle, slow touch, it felt one and the same to me.

Their hands. Their mouths. So soft and tender and gentle. They didn't rush or push me along, but lingered on every hollow as if determined to taste and stroke every inch of me from the curve of my ear to the smallest toe and find the spots that pleased me the most.

When Daire finally stroked his tongue across my pussy delicately, it made me shudder with need. I opened my legs more, pulling my knees up to open for him as much as possible. He nibbled with his lips, gently sucking on my folds. His tongue traced around my clit, sending ripples through my body. Pressure built and I could almost feel their blood rushing inside me, a hot bubbling pool of lava. I pushed up against his mouth, asking for more, and he obliged, flattening his tongue more firmly against me. Alrik sucked my nipple into the heat of his mouth, while he gently pinched the other, and suddenly the dam inside me broke. I quivered beneath them, trying not to cry out too loudly for the hotel rooms were paper thin. My mouth throbbed again and I ran my tongue around the roof of my mouth, but no fangs. Just a rising hunger.

:Again?: Daire asked, though whether he meant the question for me or for Alrik I wasn't sure. That single word vibrated with tension, raw with desperate hunger. He still touched me gently, slowly, though his own need pounded like a jackhammer in his skull. Need for my body. Need for my blood. I wasn't sure which he wanted the most.

I tightened my arm around Alrik's neck and felt for his emotions. He was more closed and contained, like a warrior who'd locked his emotions down deeply during a time of war. But he must have felt me reaching for him mentally as well as physically. He threw open that door, welcoming me in. His emotions poured through me: vicious hunger, pounding need, the same as Daire. But also protectiveness. Like a sworn knight of old, he had a stoic, almost fatalistic determination to stand guard at the door. I felt years of history and waiting in those emotions. He'd been waiting for this, waiting for me, his entire life. An agony of waiting, so many years I couldn't begin to count them. Watching others have love, watching others have their queen, sharing her blood, confidence, and trust, while he had none. For him, it was more than blood and sex. He wanted to be the *one*. The one to trust, the one to lead, my closest confidante, the one I needed the most.

I ran my hand down the planes of his back and looked into his eyes. "I need you."

He quivered against me. "Then you shall have me."

Daire didn't need an order to back up and let Alrik slide between my thighs. I was afraid for a moment that I'd upset him, made him jealous, and he'd leave, but he came up beside us, basically taking Alrik's place at my side so I could kiss and touch them both. Alrik was so big, so heavy, so strong. I thought I might panic. Maybe I should have, given my lack of experience. But his manner was so controlled, entirely focused on me and my pleasure, that I wasn't afraid. Even though I knew how much he wanted me, he didn't rush or force his way into my body. He stroked his dick against me, letting me feel his size, but using that size purely to make me feel good. And it did—he rubbed himself on my clit, a back and forth glide that made me arch beneath him, begging for more. Only then did he slowly ease inside me.

I'd always thought it would hurt, but with Daire kissing me, and Alrik moving so slowly, I didn't feel pain at all. Maybe a bit of a burn, some pressure, but it only added to the need building inside me. It felt like it took an eternity for him to slide all the way inside me, for him to lower his body down on his elbows above me. He didn't thrust at all, not yet. He just looked at me, and a faint shudder rocked his body. As if he couldn't believe he was here with me, either.

Daire stroked my cheek, turning my attention to him. "My queen, I will leave you now, but only to stand guard over you while you're both at risk. On my very life, no thrall will get past my blades tonight while you take your first Blood."

"You can't both drink from me at the same time?"

He made a low, vicious sound beneath his breath that made my inner muscles clench hard enough on Alrik that he grunted and shifted inside me. "Not until you have other Blood to stand guard over us, or you have a nest established that we know is safe. The master thrall is still out there to the north."

I'd forgotten about the watcher on the hill. The monster who'd taken my mother from me. I didn't want to feel that evil taint in my mind, the tendrils of fear that always crawled through my head when I felt that stain in the night. Especially this night.

Just thinking about that monster was enough for my subconscious to pinpoint where he was, even though I had terrible direction sense. I had no idea where "north" was, but I could feel the taint off to my left. I pushed that thought away, determined to ignore him. I threaded my fingers in Alrik's hair and focused on him.

Only then did he grind deeper against me, slowly at first, testing my tolerance. My response. His big hand slid down my hip, shifting me slightly, tipping me up against him. My breath caught in my throat. That pressure sent a throb through my core. My inner muscles clenched on that hard dick inside me and I couldn't help but shudder.

He made a low, hungry noise and slowly pulled out of me. Stars above, so slowly, I swear he felt a mile long. I grabbed at his back, trying to pull him closer, to stop that inexorably torturous glide. Just as slowly, he pushed back in to the hilt, pausing to grind his pelvis against my clit.

My heart felt like it was going to explode out of my chest. I couldn't stop tugging on him, clawing at his back, his hair, trying to pull him down to me. His mouth. I wanted his mouth. On my skin, my throat, and then it dawned on me.

I wanted his teeth.

"Please," I whispered against his lips.

His gentle control cracked. A sliver at first, with a harder, quicker thrust. Again. It was natural to arch my back, my throat, turning my head aside in invitation. He slid his palm around my nape, supporting my head, and sank his fangs into me. I gasped, shocked at the sudden white flash of pain, riding the line of pleasure that hurt so good it was almost agony. He was inside me, dick and teeth and blood. And now my blood was inside him.

He growled out a deep, vicious cry against my throat, his body plunging harder. I could feel climax building again, but this wasn't going to be gentle, swirling pleasure, but an earthquake of clenching muscle and straining flesh. I convulsed, everything inside me detonating with the force of a nuclear explosion. I forgot about trying to keep quiet so I didn't disturb the handful of guests. I even forgot about the watcher. Alrik's shoulders heaved beneath my hands, his muscles straining. I felt his climax, a flood of warmth at my core. But the pressure filling me didn't end. It was like a black hurricane filled me, swirling waters that continued to fill me, rushing in from all directions. I saw Daire, standing to my right, his eyes glowing oddly. Like the gleam of a large animal caught watching from the woods. But then even he was gone.

Shadowed winds swirled inside me, spiraling higher. I could taste Alrik's blood on my tongue again, the memory of that rich, warm blood in my mouth. I smelled sand, dry, baked earth heated for centuries by merciless suns.

"Shara."

My mother's voice. Crying, I went to her, my hands seeking her in the darkness. As soon as I touched her, I could see her clearly, as though a full moon had broken through thick clouds. I'd forgotten how beautiful she was. Her hair was dark like mine, though with more curl and shape. I had her eyes, too. Inky midnight eyes, glittering with stars.

"My daughter."

7

SHARA

om's arms wrapped around me, squeezing so hard I couldn't breathe. It felt good, though. Many a night, she'd held me against her like this, assuring me that we were safe, even though there were monsters creeping around. She smelled like I remembered, a sweet vanilla that made my heart ache.

"I've got so much to tell you," she whispered. "But first, I'm sorry. So sorry." Her voice broke and she shook against me.

"It's all right, Mom. I'm okay, and now, two men found me. They say they're Blood. My Blood. Do you know what that means?"

She blew out a long, soft breath. "Yes. That's why you're here. Why I'm allowed to see you again. You're claiming the Isador legacy."

Daire and Alrik had mentioned a legacy too, but they'd been more excited about it. Mom sounded resigned, though maybe that was my imagination. She sat down, legs crossed, so I joined her, facing her. I glanced around, trying to place where we were. Rolling hills of sand went off in all directions and a night sky gleamed with stars overhead. A crescent moon hung over a tall mountain. No, not a mountain. The sides were too perfect and steep.

A pyramid.

"I never wanted the legacy. It was a heavy burden for me. I hope the goddess takes pity on you and gives you different gifts than mine. Gifts that will be more... bearable."

I had so many questions. What kinds of gifts? How could a gift be a bad thing? Goddess? She'd never mentioned a goddess before. But I was afraid to distract her. She'd never talked to me so openly before, and deep down, I felt an urge to hurry. I sensed that time here was precious, trickling away like sands through an hourglass. I wanted her to tell me what was most important.

"When I fell in love with Alan, I thought it was an answer to my prayers. She heard my plea and gave me a way out, a life I could enjoy without the need for blood and power. The Triune even agreed to let me leave, as long as I never spoke of my heritage and never attempted to use my powers. They placed a geas upon me, so I couldn't speak of my old life at all.

"It was easy to walk away. We lived a normal life. I had a job, a husband I loved, and there wasn't the constant struggle of deciding who to award with blood. Who to punish by with-holding my blood. Who to feed me, to gain the most power. Who to ally with. Who only wanted a taste of blood to use me as their weapon. I could finally live and breathe and it was wonderful.

"Until you came to us."

Stricken, I could only stare at her mutely.

"I loved you dearly, Shara. Never doubt that. Alan was thrilled to have a daughter, but he didn't understand the risk. We'd been outside of my nest for ten years, and not once in all those years had I been hunted by thralls. I'd given up the legacy, and my power dried up quickly. But you were born with power. From the very beginning, they smelled you. They wanted you. And they hunted us mercilessly. Without my power, I could do nothing to protect you. I couldn't even tell you what hunted us, except in the most general terms, thanks to the geas."

My stomach pitched and my breathing was too rapid and shallow. I had to concentrate on breathing in and out, slowly, before I passed out.

It was my fault that my parents were dead. The monsters had truly been hunting me all along. If I hadn't been born, Mom and Dad would still be alive.

Mom squeezed my upper arms, drawing my attention to her face. She smiled, her eyes swimming with tears. "We wouldn't have traded you for the world. Alan and I would both die a thousand times if we could have you in our lives. You truly are a gift from the goddess."

I didn't feel like a gift. In fact, I felt like a fucking curse.

"It's time."

I swallowed down the bile burning up my throat. "Time for what?"

"For you to see the goddess and receive Her gifts."

"Isis?"

Mom nodded and stood, drawing me with her. "She's waiting for you."

Cold chills raced down my spine, making me shiver. "What do I do?"

Mom pointed at the pyramid. "I can't tell you."

"You did this?"

She nodded, and her lips moved, but remained tightly sealed. The geas must have kicked in. Or perhaps the goddess refused to let her tell me what to expect. Either way, it sucked. I didn't want to screw up some ritual that I'd never been taught, or insult a goddess accidentally.

I took a step toward the pyramid, but Mom suddenly threw her arms around me, squeezing me tightly one more time. "I love you."

"I love you too, Mom. I'm so sorry that you died because of me."

"I'm not. I'll never be sorry. Hurry. She says there's little time remaining and She has much to show you."

Sands shifted beneath my feet as I neared the pyramid. I glanced back one last time, and Mom raised her left hand, her right crossed her her chest. It made me feel like she still held me, even as she said goodbye. I turned back to the steep stone walls of the pyramid, impossibly old and worn. The surface was pitted by centuries of sand and wind, but when I laid my palm against the stone, it didn't budge. A low hum vibrated through my skin, energy racing up my arm, down my spine. Hairs lifted on my arms and nape. I pulled my hand away, but I still felt that charge pulsing in my body.

The door was narrow and dark, just a hole in the side of the pyramid. I took a deep breath and stepped inside, terrified stone would slide shut and lock me inside forever. A torch gleamed ahead, pulling me through the tight hallway into a chamber. I stopped, holding my breath as I looked around at the brightly colored walls. Everything gleamed, gold and jewels. Luxurious woven rugs of deep royal purple covered the floor. The walls were etched in hieroglyphs, each perfectly clear and strangely legible. I shouldn't be able to read them... but I knew what those symbols said.

I, Isis, am all that hath been that is or shall be.

Music began to play, drawing my gaze to another door on the opposite wall. She was there, waiting, I knew it. I swallowed hard, trying not to shake as I walked toward the door. Above the archway, I read, *Blood of Isis.* I had the irrational fear that all of this was a lie, and as soon as I attempted to enter the room, I'd be sucked away in a sandstorm or killed by a giant scorpion for daring to intrude. Yeah, maybe I'd watched too many *Mummy* movies. I certainly knew not to open and read aloud from any ancient texts I discovered.

A royal purple rug led to a raised dais in the center of the chamber. A woman sat on a golden throne, illuminated by squares of silvered moonlight gleaming down into the pyramid.

She wasn't larger than life, or fearsome to look at. My eyes didn't catch fire for gazing upon Her. She wore a simple white Egyptian dress, with a heavy golden collar, many tinkling bracelets, and gold and lapis ornaments held Her heavy braids coiled into an intricate pattern on her head. A crown arched above her head like massive golden horns. She held some kind of lyre on her lap and its tinkling sounds drew me closer. I almost felt like a cobra, bespelled by her snakecharmer's flute.

She could have been any beautiful woman playing in a band or walking past on the street—until She looked up at me.

My stomach pitched like the ground had suddenly fallen away beneath my feet and I was falling into an endless pit. Her dark eyes gleamed with immense power, as if She carried the tidal power of every full moon since time began.

"Daughter of Isador."

Her voice made my bones ache. My ears rang with a dull roar and I feared I wouldn't be able to hear a command and She'd kill me on the spot. I shouldn't have been worried, because when a goddess wants to tell you something, She will be heard.

"They will not be pleased that Isador still walks this earth. They will try to silence you. They will try to kill you, before you can come to full power, and certainly before you can continue my line. I send the finest warriors to you, full of powerful, burning blood. Drink them for protection and power, always keeping them near. Their blood will be a shield until you hone your own weapons and need no shield to protect you."

"They who?" When I realized I'd spoken aloud, I clamped a hand over my mouth. Eyes wide, I stared at Her, waiting for Her reaction. Would She smite me down for daring to speak in Her presence?

She made a sound, a deep, low rumble that sounded like earth growling and shifting. It took me a moment to realize She was laughing. She lifted her hand and gestured me to come closer.

"*They* are the Old Queens Who Rule, the Triune. They don't like change, and you, dear child, represent our future on this earth. They will think your birth an abomination, but you have been created by my design. When they realize fully what you are, they will hate and fear you. They will try to control you, and when that fails, they will try to kill you."

She gestured again with that come-hither lift of Her fingers, Her long nails polished gold and honed to a tip. I sidled closer, not scared, exactly, but wary. The fine hairs on my body rose, my skin tingling with the energy pouring off Her. My skull throbbed with Her power. Up close, She was even more beautiful. Her skin absolutely flawless, glowing with power, gleaming like polished obsidian and diamonds. My eyes burned as if I'd stared too long at the sun, but I couldn't look away. It hurt to be so close to Her—yet now that I'd seen Her, I never wanted to leave.

She turned her left wrist up and used one of those vicious-looking nails to puncture her skin. Crimson blood welled at the hole—but didn't spray like mine would have if I'd torn a hole in my vein. The blood didn't even look real. It was too shiny, glowing like molten lava and rubies.

"Drink, Last Child of Isador. Drink long and deep. You are the last of my line, and thus I give you *all* my gifts."

I'd practically fallen on Daire and Alrik like a starving wolf, but I hesitated to taste Her blood. If their blood had made me feel so incredible, powerful, and beautiful... what would a goddess's blood do to me?

She pressed her wrist to my mouth and I took a small sip. Afraid to take too much. Afraid to draw that much power into my body. I'd never been powerful. After a lifetime of hiding and running and fighting, I didn't know what significant power would do to me. I wanted to fight. I wanted to strike down the monsters who'd killed my mother. I'd be glad to kill them. *Glad.*

Would I start murdering people once the thralls were dead?

Would I slaughter humans for sport? I didn't think I had such evil in me, but I'd never guessed I was a vampire.

A monster.

If I fed that monster…

"So polite." Her voice a soothing sing-song whisper in my head. *"You are female. You are Isador. You've always been powerful. Think you that anyone else could have survived alone as long as you have? Take your birthright and use it. The world needs it. The world needs you."*

She folded Her other arm around me, drawing me closer into Her embrace. My skin screamed with the contact, electric shocks racing through my nervous system. I quivered, waiting for an explosion. Or maybe my brain would just shut down, all its fuses blown.

Her blood filled my mouth. But it didn't taste like copper and hot salty blood. She tasted like liquid moonlight, filtered through a bottomless lake fed by an icy-blue glacier. So cold, I could feel ice crystals on my tongue. I had a moment to feel ice spreading, numbingly cold, sealing my throat. An image flashed through my mind—me, frozen solid, buried in an avalanche. Somehow I still managed to swallow, and her blood changed from ice to sweet honeyed nectar that glowed with all the power of the sun. It melted the ice as quickly as it'd formed, spreading warmth through my body. The heat grew, as if I'd swallowed the sun itself. My insides felt tender and burned, my skin blistered. Tears sizzled on my cheeks. I tried to throw myself away from Her, but She whispered again, holding me close.

"Some of my most wondrous powers come at a steep cost. Will you pay the cost, Daughter of Isador?"

I remembered Dad, bleeding on the street, dying so I could escape. Mom's throat torn open, the monsters taunting me, trying to draw me out of the saferoom she'd locked me into. They'd paid the ultimate cost for me, so I could be here, now, receiving these gifts. The hell if I'd chicken out and waste their deaths.

I lost count of the swallows, but each one brought new

sensation, some so strong that I flinched and gasped against Her. The most surprising was burning lust. Need exploded in me. I pressed harder against Her, rubbing against Her, somehow on Her lap though I had no memory of climbing onto the throne. I had just enough brain cells left to fear that now I'd really gone and offended Her.

Until I realized She nuzzled my throat and cupped my breast. Memories poured into me, so real that it was hard to remember they hadn't actually happened to me, but to Her. Hands stroking her. Me. Hungry mouths. Male, female, both, other. It didn't matter. They all felt divine. They all wanted to touch and please the goddess.

"It's been so long."

Her voice echoed with hollowed sadness. I wanted to ask if She had no one here at the pyramid. No one to talk to, no one to touch. But I didn't want to take my mouth from Her blood, not while She still had power to send to me.

Heated desire chilled, Her blood changing again. I felt the coldness of the grave, the chill of death, an echoing endless numb sleep. My head rolled to the side awkwardly and I lost contact with the puncture wound. My body twitched and I could literally feel the light dying inside of me. Little pieces of my soul drying up, withering away. A hard gust of wind would shatter the husk and scatter me to the four directions.

I lay across her lap and died.

8

DAIRE

I was well used to watching other people have sex and being expected to stand guard and not participate. As only a minor sib, I'd never been allowed to join the queen's bed. I understood the hierarchy and my job. Shara, though, was my queen too. Damn it. *My queen.*

When Rik started feeding, it was all I could do not to come. Though our bond, I felt the tidal wave of power flooding his body. So much power. I don't know how he'd contain it all.

When he came with all the explosive power trapped inside his powerful alpha body, I almost lost it again. I wanted to come with her, inside her, feel her writhing beneath me. Even better if Rik was inside me, coming too. All of us climaxing at the same time. Again and again.

I'll have the chance soon enough.

The air was thick in the room, heavy with power and sex and blood. All the hairs on my body lifted, my skin tingling. I could smell the tantalizing rich scent of her blood, mixed with sex, and I couldn't wait any longer. I took a step closer to the bed.

A vicious howl tore through the night, breaking through my

moment of weakness. I whirled around and grabbed my ketars, ready to tear the thrall apart if he even thought about trying to step foot into this flimsy roach motel she called home. Reaching out with my senses, I felt the dark, foul stains on the night. Multiple human thralls roamed outside the hotel, whipped into a desperate frenzy by their master's hunger. They knew well that two Blood had found her. Die facing Blood, or die when they returned to the master empty handed? They didn't have much choice. At least I would give them a quick and merciful death.

Evidently the memory of the attack where we'd easily killed several of their kind was fresh enough in their minds that they chose to return to their master. They pulled back, slinking away like starving coyotes, but the thrall still howled off in the distance. I felt his rage. His desperate hunger. His need.

For my queen. Same as me.

I would kill for her too.

Pity flickered through me. Not enough to spare his life if and when he came after Shara, but understanding. Not much separated me from him in the end. If she died, and didn't resolve our bond beforehand, I, too would roam the night killing like a mindless, starving beast, desperate to find myself a new queen. Though no queen would take a thrall as Blood.

A ragged groan sent me wheeling back to the bed. That masculine sound wasn't one of pleasure, but pain. I'd never heard Rik whimper.

But he wasn't Rik any longer. A huge hulking shape rose up over Shara, impossibly wide. Like a mountain. Fuck. He'd come into his power—and shifted into something I'd never seen before.

Blood were generally able to transform into protective predators: wolves, lions, panthers, even a few dragons back in the old days. But this... He looked like a rock troll. Literally, his muscles and limbs looked like giant boulders.

"Shara!" His voice sounded like an earthquake mixed with an explosion. He turned and looked at me over his shoulder.

There was nothing of the man I knew in that face, except his eyes. Those eyes I knew. And he was fucking terrified. "Something's wrong. I think she's dead."

I scrambled to the side of the bed and checked her pulse. Nothing. Her eyes were open but unseeing and glassy. I pressed my ear to her chest, and I couldn't hear her heart beating. Even her skin was starting to chill.

I started chest compressions and gave her mouth-to-mouth for several cycles, then checked her heart and pulse again. "No. Shara. No!"

Rik slid a giant platter-sized palm behind her neck and lifted her slightly, checking the wounds he'd made with his fangs. Neat, tidy, and though I'd been too aroused myself to pay attention to how long he drank, I doubted he could have drained her to the point of death. I'd never heard of a Blood being able to drain his queen to death with a single feeding.

Dread certainty filled me. I'd been afraid she might revive an entire cemetery, but maybe her greatest power would be resurrecting herself. I whispered, "Remember who she is."

"Isador," Rik ground out in that rumbling new voice. "House of Isis."

"The goddess of resurrection. I could continue chest compressions, but I don't want to risk breaking her ribs for no reason."

Rik gingerly stepped off the bed, though why he bothered I couldn't say. The frame was already a pile of kindling, the mattress on the floor. He sat on the floor, drew her lifeless body into his arms, and then held a hand out to me. "We should hold her. Keep her close and warm and safe."

I took his hand and settled into his arms with her. Rik held us both easily, as if we were just children. I wrapped my arms around her and put my head against her chest so I'd hear the first beat of her heart. Though with the low roar of his breathing, I'd be lucky to hear a jet taking off. "Can you shift back now?"

He grunted and it sounded like a piece of the earth tearing away in a landslide. "Not until she's safe. If we have to fight our way out…"

"Then at least stop with the earthquake and rumbling boulder sounds so I can hear, big guy."

He quit making the sound, and the resulting silence was deafening. I guess he was holding his breath. "How long—"

I cut off that sentence, straining to hear. I heard a trickle, a rustle, almost like the brush of feathers, or a lock of hair lifting in the breeze. The barest flap of silk. I burrowed closer to her, wrapping my body around hers. "Come back to us, Shara."

SHARA

KNOWING that I was dead was worse than actually *being* dead, if that made sense. Death was empty, silent, cold blackness, like the depths of the universe with all the stars blown out. I didn't see any guiding light bringing me back. I didn't see loved ones in the distance beckoning me to paradise. Just… darkness.

The thought of an eternity like this made me scream—even though I couldn't hear it and didn't have any vocal chords.

I whirled, or at least tried to look around, but there was nothing to see. Just endless, black emptiness.

It wasn't supposed to end this way. Was it? Why had Mom given birth to me against all hope, and died to keep me safe, if I was going to die here alone? Isis had given me power. Great power, supposedly. Power over life and death.

If I didn't want death… then I had to choose life. But how?

The power had to be *within* me. Inside. Not out.

Instead of blindly searching the invisible horizons in this nothingness, I looked inward. I felt deep inside myself, gliding past memories and thoughts. I saw Daire and Alrik running toward me as I lifted the knife to my throat. I felt a tug in my memory and paused to look. I followed through the woods to the top of a hill. Moonlight shone down on a clearing, illuminating a man with long silvered hair. He looked up at me, his eyes widening as if he could see me too. The man who'd killed my mother looked much worse for wear in the five years since she'd died. His face was sunken hollows and dark flaming eyes. He bared a vicious stained row of pointy teeth and leaped at me. In slow motion, I watched his bony, gnarled hand come closer, each finger tipped with brutal black claws. But I wasn't afraid.

I knew I could disintegrate him into dust with a thought.

I pushed his image away and searched deeper. I saw Dad lifting me up onto his shoulders, his eyes worried as he checked the sinking sun, but he kept his voice light, his manner happy. He didn't want to scare me. Mom rocking me against her, singing something soft and low in a language I recognized but hadn't understood at the time. After visiting the goddess's pyramid, I knew those Egyptian words. *"You are my sunshine"*, sang in her native language. Despite knowing she'd die because of me.

"Not because *of you,"* Mom whispered in my head. *"For you. Gladly."*

"Why?" I asked, not sure that she could hear me.

"Because I love you."

Love. That single word sparked something inside me. A chip of heat, a tiny ember, glowing like a miniature sun. As I focused on it, the flame burned a bit brighter. So beautiful, so pure. A drop of molten sunlight. It expanded inside me, illuminating my stilled heart, blood heavy and cold in my veins. One touch of that brightness melted the blood and warmed my heart. I felt it beat, a heavy, echoing thud. So slow, but strong.

With a huge gasping breath, I jerked upright. My chest ached, my heart thumping frantically like it was trying to escape my chest.

"I've got you. We're here. You're safe."

Daire. I felt his skin on mine, his heat wrapped around me. I couldn't seem to make my eyes work yet, but something banded me to him. Something granite-hard and cold. That moved when I touched it. My mind recognized him, sensing his immense relief through the bond we'd formed. "Alrik? What's wrong?"

"Nothing, my queen, not now that you're back."

His voice rumbled like a massive thundercloud tearing through the room. It made my eyes flare open wide. I looked at the massive... thing... holding both of us and the only thing I could say was, "Oh. My."

Daire laughed. "I think he's a rock troll. Hot, huh?"

Alrik did look like a giant boulder-man. I laid my hand on his chest and felt stone, not skin or flesh. "Actually, he's cold."

I felt something in the bond with him. A tightening, as if he was withdrawing, or hiding. I reached for his thoughts and realized he was afraid.

Afraid I'd be disgusted by this new shape. Or worse, afraid of him. Trolls were nasty creatures who lived beneath bridges, or ate people they kidnapped. His stomach was a mess of churning acid, rather than joy at finally coming into his power, because he was afraid I wouldn't want to touch him or look at him using the very gift my blood had given him.

Stupid man.

I thought that at him very hard, making sure he heard it. His eyes narrowed but he said nothing.

I rose up on my knees, bracing myself on one of his gigantic thighs the size of a Sequoya tree trunk. Even then, I had to reach up for his face, stretching to touch him. He obligingly bent down to me and I cupped his cheeks in my palms. Then I very deliberately locked my mouth to his.

His lips were hard and cold, too large to kiss me back without covering most of my jaw, but he relaxed into my hands, sinking his face deeper into my caress. I traced the shape of his stone lips with my tongue and his breath exhaled on a low rumbling purr that vibrated my bones.

Daire pressed against my back, tucking me against the solid wall of Alrik's chest. "We feared for you."

At his words, Alrik shuddered against me and pressed his forehead to mine. "You died in my arms. It was the most horrible thing I've ever lived through."

"It wasn't pleasant for me either," I said wryly. "I guess that's what you meant by a curse."

"Everyone's heard rumors of House Isador's deadly gifts," Alrik said grimly. "And no one was missing Isador the past thirty years."

The crushing weight of this new legacy was going to take some getting used to. "*She*," I said with emphasis, because it felt disrespectful to use the goddess's given name, "said they would try to kill me. Is that true?"

When they both tightened their arms around me, I had my answer before Alrik said, "Yes."

"But that's what we're here for," Daire said, rubbing his cheek against my shoulder.

I could feel Alrik in my mind, his touch solid, steady, protective, alert. I felt his emotions as my own. Relief that I was alive, anger at the thought of anyone trying to hurt me, and yeah, desire. The big guy was already hard and thinking about sex again, though I couldn't feel his erection when his entire body was a chunk of concrete.

I couldn't feel Daire the same way, even though he was tight against my back. I didn't have a full bond with him. Yet. I looked up at Alrik. Smiling, he carefully drew one of his large fingers down my cheek. "You have another Blood to take, my queen."

Daire didn't say anything or move, but I felt his intensity ratchet up a notch. Hunger. Desire. Desperate aching need. I didn't need a bond to know how much he wanted my blood, and my body, the same as his friend had done.

I turned my head toward him, and that was enough encouragement for him to lift and turn me fully around to face him.

He smiled, a dimple flashing in his cheek. "Hi."

Fuck, he was sexy as hell. "Did you want something?"

He nodded vigorously, his hair tumbled down into his eyes. "Yes, my queen."

"What do you want?"

His smile slipped, his eyes wide and dark as he stared at me. "You."

"But how?"

He shook his head slightly. "You. The rest doesn't matter."

I reached out to play with his hair, twirling one of the touseled locks around my finger as I tried to figure him out. He liked to joke around, that was obvious. He could flirt one second, and be deadly serious the next. He was just as protective as Alrik, but not as … driven or solemn or intense. He could take things lighter, because he trusted Alrik to have things under control.

"I'm his alpha," Alrik whispered against my ear. Very human lips. I hadn't felt or sensed him changing back into his normal shape. There hadn't been any flash of light or even a hair prickling on my skin. "Now you're his alpha too."

"Am I your alpha?"

"You're my queen. You're so far beyond alpha that if you ordered me to cease breathing, I'd die trying."

But there was an element of… not pride, exactly, but steel, in his manner. He would take my orders, probably even gladly, because he chose to do it. Even before he'd gained his troll power, he'd possessed that steel in his spine, the weight in his words, the directness in his manner. Yet they'd said they'd never served a queen before. It must have chaffed his pride for years to be so far removed from the queen, the primary source of power in his world.

A normal man would probably get ideas in his head about how quickly he could overthrow the woman and take control for himself. I didn't sense that kind of drive in him—only a determination to take care of me. He was the kind of man who'd fight to the death, even if stark naked and unarmed. Protecting me.

Dying for me.

That made me shudder. I'd only known them a few hours, but I couldn't imagine going back to my old life. Always alone. Moving. Scared. Lonely. Aching for comfort and safety.

:Never again, Shara. You'll never be alone again.:

I realized that even if I was physically separated from Alrik, I still wouldn't be alone, because he'd be in my head. He'd know what I was feeling or thinking. It should have felt intrusive, like a violation of my privacy, but at least right now, I actually liked it. I liked having his touch, even if only in my mind.

And I really wanted Daire to have that same ability. I looked into his eyes and watched the way his pupils dilated, his nostrils flaring.

"Take me to bed."

9

SHARA

He scooped me up into his arms and climbed into bed, still holding me in his arms. Lying flat on his back, he looked up at me and quirked his luscious mouth. "I'm at your disposal, my queen."

I'd never straddled a man like this. Even sitting on his stomach, I could feel the ridges of muscle beneath me. I squirmed a little, drinking in the feel of so much power and strength beneath me. Then I squirmed some more when I noticed the way his breathing caught.

I smoothed my palms across the planes of his chest, his powerful shoulders. His skin felt like warm silk over steel.

"I taste even better."

I arched a brow at him. "Is that an invitation or an order?"

Until I said it, I hadn't registered the difference. Not really. I'd never thought about giving orders to anyone. All I'd worried about was hiding, staying alive, living to fight another day. Even when Alrik had said he was Daire's alpha. That I was even higher than that. It hadn't made sense.

Until I had Daire beneath me. Until I thought about *him* telling *me* to do something.

And something inside me rejected that notion. Whole-heartedly.

"Neither. Only the most sincere and humble plea, my queen."

That made me snort. Daire might be a laughing, teasing jokester, but there wasn't anything *humble* about him.

I leaned down and pressed my mouth to his pectoral. I meant to kiss him, maybe tease him a little with my tongue. But once I felt his skin against my mouth, I wanted to bite. My teeth throbbed again. I wanted so badly to sink fangs into him, to feel his skin give way beneath me. To taste the hot surge of blood in my mouth.

Though I was afraid I'd bite him again and again.

:He'd like nothing better,: Alrik said in my head. *:Neither would I.:*

I gripped that heavy muscle in my jaws, holding his flesh in my mouth. I pressed harder, willing my fangs to come out, but nothing happened. Groaning with frustration, I released him with my very human teeth. "When am I going to be able to bite you like I want?"

His chest heaved and he gripped my thighs. "Still feels good. Bite me some more."

I gripped the column of his throat in my teeth, pressing slightly harder and harder until his fingers tightened on my thighs. I ran my teeth down the side of his throat with a light scrape. The thick muscle running across his shoulder was next. I opened my mouth as wide as I could, gripping him firmly, and I couldn't hold back a possessive growl.

It startled me enough I let him go and even sat back a little. I felt... feral. Desire purred and rumbled inside me, hunger rising, and it wasn't just for sex. Something about him made me want to growl and bite and scratch.

He made a low, rumbling growl too, very much like a giant cat. I had a feeling that his power would indeed be some kind of feline. With his tousled hair and glowing eyes, I could easily see him walking as a lion. Or a sleek panther, prowling through the night.

"Rik," he panted, staring up at me. "Would you please fucking bite me so she can taste me again?"

I felt Alrik's touch on the bond, a hint of question, though not words. He didn't want to interrupt my time with Daire, unless I wanted it.

"Yes, please." I sat up, lifting my hips so I could move down Daire's body. His dick twitched as I passed over him, as if it had a homing device focused on my pussy. "I want to taste you both again."

The mattress dipped as Alrik joined us. He stretched out beside Daire, leaning down over him. Broad shoulders, ripped muscles, but his touch was gentle as he cupped Daire's nape and lifted his throat to his mouth.

Daire gasped, his hips arching up beneath me. His cock surged, desperate, and I couldn't wait any longer. I took him inside me as Alrik fed, and all I could picture was the three of us, bleeding, fucking, touching each other. All night long.

"Fuck, yes, soon," Alrik groaned, lifting his head. "But not until you're well guarded."

Daire jerked up toward me, wrapping his arms around me. The scent of his blood drew me like a magnet. I licked the blood from his skin, letting it lead me to the punctures in the side of his throat. Subconsciously, I couldn't help but worry about so much blood. I'm sure we were staining the bed linens, the carpet, hell, maybe even the ceiling for all I knew. But the more I touched and tasted and saw their blood, the more I wanted. It was foreplay, appetizer, and main meal all in one, especially with his dick inside me. I turned my head away and rubbed myself against him, smearing blood on my throat and shoulder. It felt good.

Damned good.

I suddenly wondered if his blood was somehow addictive, a

drug that I was absorbing through my skin. I certainly felt buzzed. My ears throbbed with the thunder of our hearts. The scent of blood and desire and semen stirred my hunger even more. Daire rocked his hips, stroking deep inside me, his mouth on my breast. Blindly, I reached out for Alrik, tugging him closer. I knew he wanted to remain aloof and on guard, but I wanted his touch. I wanted his heat against me.

He drew my mouth to his, supporting my head. Daire gripped my hips, lifting me, pulling me, urging me higher. I knew what a release felt like, now. I knew that it was close. I wanted it. Needed it.

And I wanted Daire's bite when I came.

I don't know which came first, his bite or my climax. Maybe Alrik told him through the bond what I wanted, but Daire timed it perfectly. He sank his fangs into me and I shattered. It felt like I had wings, soaring higher and higher into a midnight sky, only to burst into a thousand shining lights.

Awareness came back in pieces. My head was on Alrik's chest. I smelled his scent of smoke and iron. A heavy weight lay across my legs. I thought it was his thigh, or maybe Daire's. But then I realized it wasn't skin against me, but fur.

Blinking my eyes open, I lifted my head. A massive striped black cat lay across my lower legs and against my side, tail lashing back and forth playfully. Large golden eyes met mine and his mouth opened to reveal vicious fangs. He was larger than any cat I'd ever seen. Like a saber tooth tiger on steroids.

Alrik stroked his hand through my hair and I nestled back into his embrace. Daire rubbed his giant head against my side, until I draped my arm across his shoulders. "Do you know what he is?"

:Warcat,: Daire said in my head, his mental voice a deep rumbling purr.

I started to laugh. I couldn't help it. He licked my flank, his tongue a giant piece of sandpaper that made me gasp. "Sorry. I just realized I went from a simple, everyday human a few hours ago, to learning I'm a vampire and having sex with a giant rock troll and furry warcat. That's all kinds of fucked up. Uh... literally."

Alrik laughed, tightening his arm around me. "You haven't seen anything yet."

10

SHARA

I'd forgotten the luxury of having someone to talk to when you first woke up in the morning. Sunlight streamed in through the cracks around the ugly hotel drapes, but I couldn't tell what time it was. My stomach growled. Loudly.

Snickering, Daire untangled his limbs and brushed his mouth against mine. "Good morning, my queen. Your alarm clock has pronounced it's time to get up."

He started to pull back, but I leaned up, kissing him more fully, and he was only too happy to oblige. I came up for air. "Why does my stomach growl for food if I'm a vampire?"

"We eat food for our bodies. Blood for our power." Alrik kissed my shoulder. "What would you like for breakfast? Daire will grab something while I help you pack."

I let my head fall back and Daire started gathering up his clothes. "Where are we going?"

"Do you have a safe house? A nest? Anywhere you feel especially safe?"

I couldn't help but watch Daire pull jeans up his solid thighs, and I sighed with regret when he covered up his incredible ass. He winked at me over his shoulder. "I've never felt safe. I don't stay in any place for long. Three weeks, usually. Sometimes two, sometimes four. It depends on how quickly they find me."

"I'll never cease to be amazed at how incredibly lucky we are that you're still alive." Alrik didn't sound amazed—he sounded pissed. "Where did you live with Selena? Before she died?"

I stroked my fingers over his forearm, searching for where he'd torn his wrist for me last night. But there wasn't even a scar. I had a quivering moment of doubt that my half-human genes wouldn't allow me to heal as quickly, but I felt my throat where I'm sure he'd bitten me last night, and the skin was completely smooth. Amazing. "We had a big old house in Kansas City."

"That's where we should start. We need to find your consiliarius."

"My what?"

Alrik pulled away and joined the hunt for his clothes too. "Each royal house has a steward, a... lawyer, I guess you would call it. A trustee. Someone who manages the legacy for his or her queen."

"I've got a few choice words for the Isador consiliarius, if we can find the bastard." Daire shot a dark look at Alrik, who nodded back. "It's intolerable that you've been lost this long. That you've had no access to the legacy or your family's wealth. How have you lived alone this long? Food, shelter, transportation?"

"I work when I can." I shrugged, avoiding their gazes while I sat up and looked about the room. Daire turned the light on and I groaned with dismay. The room was a disaster. Blood stained the carpet and the linens, and the cheap hotel furniture looked like it'd been tossed about by a tornado. The mattress was on the floor, the frame shattered. The end table was kindling and the flat-screen television looked like someone had hit it repeatedly with a baseball bat. Even the walls looked battered and fragile, ready to collapse under the weight of the roof. "Oh God. When did all this happen?"

Daire tugged on his boots. "When you came into your power."

I groaned and buried my face in my hands. "It's going to take forever to clean the blood out of the carpet, and the last of my savings to pay Hosea back for the damage."

Alrik closed his hands over mine and pulled my hands away. "No. It won't. First of all, the Isador legacy is rich enough that you could buy this whole state if you wanted to."

"But—"

He leaned down, a fierce look in his eyes. "You're the fucking queen of Isador and you clean nothing. You pay for nothing. You worry for nothing. This damage is nothing. We will take care of it."

"But—"

He pressed his lips to mine in a hard, searing kiss. Goosebumps raced down my arms and my inner muscles clenched. It'd be very easy to lie back on the mattress and pull him down with me. My stomach gurgled again, so hungry for food, his blood, and his body that I couldn't tell which I wanted more.

"Trust us," he whispered against my mouth. "I swear on your sweet blood burning in my veins that there's nothing we can't take care of in your service. Absolutely nothing."

Trust wasn't something that came easily to me. I'd never had anyone but my parents to rely on, and they'd been gone a long time. I took a deep breath and let it out slowly. My brain still whirled frantically about the best way to get blood out of the carpet, but I nodded.

"I'll pack your things. Just tell me where everything is."

I pointed to the backpack by the door. "That's it."

He looked at the single bag and Daire winced.

Alrik tightened his grip on the bedding and something ripped in protest, but his voice was even when he spoke. "Very well. We'll get you dressed and get the hell out of this fucking town. As Isis is my witness, we're taking you shopping in New York and Paris as soon as possible."

66

I'd never been out of the Midwest, let alone the country. I still couldn't get my mind wrapped around the idea of having that kind of money, rather than cleaning rooms just to have a roof over my head, but I let it slide. "I should jump in the shower first."

"There's no need," Daire said as he grabbed my bag and last night's clothes so I could decide what to wear. "You're bathed in power now."

Bathed in power? What? I looked down at my self and cringed. Blood splattered my skin and I felt gummy and sticky between my thighs. I should have gotten up in the night and cleaned up—

Alrik gave my shoulders a gentle shake. "My queen cleans nothing, even herself."

"But—"

"Last night, how did you seek us that first time? Before we reached you?"

Unsure what that had to do with anything, I answered slowly, "I imagined the area around me like a tapestry in my mind."

"Go there in your mind now. Picture this room as the tapestry."

I closed my eyes and brought up the internal map of my surroundings. Involuntarily, I gasped. We glowed. We glowed so brightly it hurt my inner eye to look. Daire and Alrik were the deep, rich hue of molten lava and red-hot embers, and I gleamed with a soft pearly light that spun rainbows out in all directions. For miles and miles. Before they'd found me, I'd only been able to feel a few miles out, but now... I swear I could see the Missouri border, without even trying. A spot on the tapestry gleamed like a tiny candle in the window. I knew without touching it that was my childhood home in Kansas City more than two hundred miles away.

"See the blood in this room," Alrik whispered. "The drops

shine like jewels. If you touch one, you'd know whose blood it was."

I pulled my awareness back to our vicinity, but it took me a few moments to see past the glowing lights to the droplets of ruby blood. They did glow like priceless jewels. I concentrated on one and I could taste Daire, feel his fur rubbing against me.

"Draw that blood into yourself. Pull it to you. Gather it up like you're picking flowers, or calling birds home to roost. Our blood is yours to command. It will come to your call."

With my eyes closed, I opened my arms and turned slowly, basking in our brilliant light. It was like dancing naked in a clearing beneath a full moon, incredibly liberating and exciting. The droplets of blood rose, dancing around me like ruby-red butterflies. They swirled for me, wove patterns in the air, and when I dropped my arms, the blood butterflies swarmed into my light.

I quivered, feeling the impact of that power in our shared blood. Even old and dark stains still carried power.

"Let the power roll through you. Imagine it pulling away anything impure that you don't want to be on your body."

The power was already washing down my body, as if it'd known what I wanted before Alrik had given me the idea. I could feel the prickle of energy racing down my skin, head to toe, and yes, I did feel cleaner. I opened my eyes and pushed my hair back. It was full and floating about my head, as if I'd loaded it with static electricity. "Um, wow."

"Some queens can change their appearance that way—though it's said to take a great deal of blood."

The slight grim edge in Alrik's voice told me that "great" didn't mean a single feeding. In fact, he implied... violence. Maybe even murder. "Like Elizabeth Bathory?"

"Indeed. The Magyar was well pleased with Her daughter. Since her death, her house has never been the same."

I wasn't surprised that some of our kind had been evil. The touch of power still hummed on my skin, making me feel alive and full of energy. My hair had never been silkier. I felt like I could leap tall buildings and outrun thoroughbreds after tasting my two Blood. How much more power would I gain as I fed from them daily? What if others came? How much power would I gain? It gave me pause and sent a chill down my spine.

I had no illusions about human nature, let alone my own nature. I'd had my fill of hiding and running from the monsters. If I had a chance to fight, I'd take them on. I'd take them all on. If a queen came after me, I'd take her on too. I wasn't going to let anyone take this newfound power from me, certainly never take my Blood from me. I'd fight for what was mine.

And if I gained more and more power each time I fed...

I had no idea what kind of monster I was capable of becoming.

ALRIK

MY QUEEN LEARNED QUICKLY. Her skin glowed with vitality, her hair flowing like black silk over her shoulders, her body strong and proud. She pulled on jeans and a shapeless hoodie, but even covered in plain human clothes, she reeked of royal power. Pride swelled in my chest and I couldn't find the words to tell her how thankful I was that she'd called us to her side. Instead, I sent her a surge of emotion through our bond, surrendering my mind to hers. It was the greatest gift I could offer, short of laying down my life for hers.

Her stomach growled again, making Daire laugh. "Hurry up, Rik. We've got to feed her before she tears us limb from limb to satisfy that hunger."

She checked the pockets of the jeans she'd worn last night, found the pocketknife she'd carried, and slipped it into her jeans. That knife was so fucking small I wouldn't even call it a blade. "So what are we called exactly? Just vampires?"

I scanned the room, looking for anything she might have missed, but she'd kept her things in a single bag. She didn't even have a hairbrush or toothbrush in the bathroom. I could only imagine the number of times she'd had to flee, leaving behind her things. "We're Aima, the ancient blood of Gaia. All royal houses descend from the Great Mother."

Daire picked up her bag and we headed to the door. She looked back into the room, nibbling on her lip. "Hosea was really nice to me. I hate to leave him such damage to fix."

I took her hand and tucked her arm around mine. Daire went ahead and on outside to our bikes. I stopped at the concierge desk.

A young woman looked up from her phone and her eyes widened as she looked back and forth between us. By her reaction, it wasn't every day she saw a man of my size. Let alone with her friend. "Shara?"

"Hey, Ellie," she replied, blushing. "I'm taking off with some friends. Can you let Hosea know?"

"Oh, no. Sure. I'll let him know." She glanced back at me, and if possible, her eyes got even larger. "Does he owe you anything? It's almost Christmas. I'm sure he'd give you a little extra for a bonus if you could stick around."

"No, sorry, I really need to head out. I'm really really sorry, but there's a bit of a mess…"

I started to lay hundred-dollar bills on the counter and Shara fell silent. Now her eyes were as big as the other woman's and that pissed me off all over again. She acted like she'd never seen that much money in her life, when she had to be one of the richest queens alive. The Isador legacy had always been immense, and without her mother drawing on it the last thirty plus years, it had to have grown astronomical, unless the consiliarius was a complete idiot. Which I would believe, unfortunately, since Shara had been lost for so long.

"I broke a few things." I tried to keep my rage out of my words, but Shara pressed against me, as if her presence could still my anger. And it did. "I forget how big I am sometimes. I'm a complete bull-in-a-china-cabinet. Please convey my apologies to Mr. Hosea. I believe this should be enough to compensate him for the inconvenience."

"Oh. Oh. Yes. Uh. Yeah."

I laid another hundred-dollar bill on the counter and pushed it to the young woman. "Thank you, and Merry Christmas."

Her eyes filled with tears, and I suddenly wished I'd given her two or three bills. "Bye, Shara. Good luck."

The roar of a motorcycle engine made Shara jump. "Thanks, Ellie. Bye."

We headed outside. Daire was already seated, revving his engine. "What sounds good to eat? My queen, what's wrong? Why is she crying?"

I pulled her to me, alarm rising, tightening my throat. Had I offended her? Hurt her? Neglected her in some way? I hadn't felt any dismay through the bond, but I might have missed something while indulging in my own anger.

"Thank you," she whispered, her voice shaking. "That was really sweet. A hundred dollars will be the difference between her having a nice Christmas and maybe not having enough to eat when Hosea has to lay her off."

Relieved, I lifted her up onto my bike so she'd sit in front of me. She might rather hold on to me against my back—but I'd die before I left my queen's back unprotected. I helped her with her helmet. Daire tossed me my leather jacket and I tugged it on and buckled my helmet. I didn't need either for protection—I doubted even a horrific accident would kill me—but it helped us avoid attention if we dressed like humans and followed their laws. "I can run back in and give her more. This is nothing, Shara. Honestly, you should have tens of millions times such a paltry sum."

"No, if you take more to her, it'll wound her pride. It's still a windfall for her."

I climbed on behind her, enfolding her against me. She was

small enough that I'd have no problem seeing around her, and I'd serve as a windbreak at the same time. I started up the bike and let her get used to the way it rumbled beneath us.

She lifted her head, stretching up toward my neck, so I leaned down to hear her. "What kind of bike is this?"

"Harley."

"I like it." I started to sit back up, but something in the bond made me hesitate, listening, waiting. "Would it be too much to ask for a leather jacket like yours?"

I licked her throat beneath the rim of the helmet and grazed her skin with my teeth. "Nothing's too much for my queen. If you want a jacket coated in diamonds and rubies, we'll get it."

She curled up against me like a kitten. "No jewels. Just leather. I like the way it smells. Almost as good as you."

Daire raised his voice over the rumbling engines. "Where to, my queen?"

"Mom's old safe house was in Kansas City." She gave us an image of the map she carried in her head, with the candle flame to the north. "I think we should start there."

Daire tore off immediately, leaving a black streak on the grayed concrete parking lot. I pulled out more leisurely, very aware of the precious cargo I carried with me.

My queen. Mine. After so long.

She wriggled back against me tighter and wrapped her palms around my biceps. Exhilaration burned in her bond. She'd never ridden a motorcycle. She'd never gone anywhere without worrying about her safety. :*Can we go faster?*:

Without answering, I blew past Daire. We flew down the curving, winding road that led out of Eureka Springs.

My queen leaned forward into the wind and lifted her hands out to the side, her glorious laughter like a spur to my flank, urging me to push well past the speed limit.

Stupid? Yeah. Reckless? Hell yeah.

It was going to be a brutal ride with this massive of a hard-on.

11

SHARA

I lifted my head from Alrik's chest as we neared my mother's house. We'd stopped only for pancakes and a quick shopping trip in Springfield, Missouri, where he bought me the softest, most delicious smelling leather jacket. I still felt guilty about spending his money, though every time my conscience twinged, he glared at me. I didn't need it for warmth, but the weight of it across my shoulders felt good. I'd managed to doze off the last hour or two. Evidently even Isis's last queen needed to sleep now and then after a night of sex.

My heartbeat quickened as we entered my old neighborhood. Despite being only a short drive from downtown Kansas City, Stuller had a small-town vibe with fields, small farms, and green space. Most of the town had fallen by the wayside over the years, even more so since I'd left five years ago. The old abandoned church had actually fallen down and was only a pile of rubble beside some leaning grayed tombstones from the 1800s. We passed the park where I'd played softball until Dad's death, now an overgrown field dotted with junk cars. Large old trees lined the road we turned down. No other houses were on this street, so we didn't pass any cars. As far as I remembered, we were the only house, our yard bordering the back of the park. The house had been old, though grand, five years ago. I couldn't imagine that it'd fared well in the years since I'd left.

But as we slowed at the iron gate, I couldn't tell that a single year had passed. The lawns still looked well manicured, the street and private driveway were clean of debris. The old house looked the same: huge square tower, red brick exterior, doors and windows intact.

"Have you never come back to this house?" Alrik asked.

I shook my head. "I was too scared. The monsters knew I had lived here. I thought they'd leave a lookout, or know immediately if I came back."

Involuntarily, my head turned to the right, my eyes searching down the dead-end road that went past the house. Even at high noon, the end of the road was cloaked in shadows. I knew the park lay on the other side. That had been the shortcut. The place my father, and then my mother, had been killed. Would I feel something of her there? Would her blood still resonate, like ours had gleamed in the hotel room? Or had the monsters sucked every last bit of her blood out of the concrete? Where had she been buried? I had no idea.

Daire rattled the gate. "It's locked. I could tear it down if you want, but let's try the intercom."

"Someone had to have bought the house," I said. "It doesn't look abandoned."

He shrugged. "It's worth a shot. If nothing else, they'll know who they bought the house from, and that should give us someone in charge of your mother's estate."

"Your consiliarius," Alrik clarified. "There should be someone running the Isador legacy for you, until you come into power and claim your birthright."

Daire hit the call button. I found myself breathing more quickly. Afraid no one would answer. Afraid someone would. Mom had never said a word about a consiliarius. But maybe she couldn't. What if I could have had someone to arrange things for me all along? If I hadn't had to starve and work shady under-the-table jobs, constantly on the run? But how could I have known? And could this person even be trusted?

"Good afternoon, Talbott Agency." A woman's voice came through the speaker. "Can I help you?"

The only word Daire said was, "Isador."

"Hold please. Ms. Talbott will be right with you."

Anxious, I shivered slightly. Alrik tightened his arms around me, dropping his chin on top of my head. "Are you sure we can trust whoever Ms. Talbott is?"

"No," Alrik replied. "But this is where we start. If we don't like her answers, your warcat can eat her."

Daire's eyes lit up and he made a playful slash with his hand. It made me laugh—exactly as they intended. I knew by now that they didn't go around hurting people. Only monsters who tried to hurt me.

"I will kill anyone, human or thrall or beast, who tries to hurt you," Alrik whispered against my ear. "I won't stay my hand for anyone but you."

His words sent a warm flood through me. It shouldn't have felt so good to hear him threaten to kill people. But it did. It felt very good to know I had him at my back. That I didn't have to fight the monsters alone any longer.

"Good afternoon, this is Gina Talbott," a woman said through the speaker, her words hurried. "Can you repeat that word please?"

"Isador," Daire said.

"Is Shara with you? Is she all right?"

"I'm here," I raised my voice to be sure it carried through the intercom. "Who are you?"

"Blessed be! Stay there, please, Your Majesty. I'll be there in fifteen minutes."

Crap. I guess she knew a thing or two after all. "I don't think I'm ever going to get used to anyone calling me that."

Fifteen minutes. Guess that was long enough to face my

fears. I looked at Daire and he immediately came closer and took my hand, helping me step off Alrik's motorcycle. He kept my hand, and Alrik took my other. They knew without asking what I wanted to do.

I led them down to the shadowed dead-end cul-de-sac. Massive trees blocked the sun and the wind. Old wet leaves made a thick carpet on the concrete. But as we neared the end of the road, I could feel a spot that didn't feel right. Old pain lingered here. Death.

I dragged my gaze to the trees, refusing to look down, afraid to see my mother's murder play out again. The footpath through to the park was overgrown, but still there as I remembered. "We cut through there to get to the park, rather than walking down the street to the front entrance. Dad called it our secret gate. They killed him, right here, and then they killed Mom too." I looked back up at the house. The iron fence wrapped around the back of the property. *"Always use iron,"* she'd said. I still remembered her sprinkling salt around the fence too, every single month.

My two men enfolded me between them. I breathed in their scents, soaked in their heat, rested on their strength. I felt their steady touch in my mind, our bond forged by blood and trust. While they held me, I stretched out my hand toward the spot where my parents had died, and let them see what had happened.

I PRESSED AGAINST THE TINY, dirty basement window, desperate to see what was happening. My hands ached from pounding on the door, but the heavy oak hadn't even cracked. I could bust out the glass... but the window was too small for me to get through. It was barely more than a peephole. But I saw everything.

Mom walked down the path from our backyard to the iron gate. Head high, shoulders back, she didn't rush or tremble with fear, despite the shrieks and howls from the monsters waiting in the trees. A huge yard light illumi-

nated the gate—our weak spot in our defenses. Dad had joked that we could get suntans at night if we sat under the light for too long. The monsters certainly didn't like it.

"Bring her to me, my love, and I'll let the human live." Even safe in the house, the creature's voice made goose bumps race down my arms. I shuddered, clutching my hands over my ears. His voice had an agonizing quality, like fingernails on a chalkboard.

Mom's hand rose to the heavy lock and chain keeping the monster at bay, and I howled as loudly as the monsters, shouting at her to stay. She heard me, and even looked back at me. She mouthed something to me, but I couldn't hear or understand what she said. Then she stepped outside the iron fence.

The monsters didn't fall on her all at once. She stopped, still in the circle of light, and waited for him to come to her. I saw his long shining hair the color of moonlight and his blood-red eyes. Now that I knew what we were, it made sense that the monster struck at her throat. He was feeding from her. And she let him—because she knew him.

I BLINKED THE VISION AWAY. "I never realized that she knew him. Why did he kill her? She let him feed."

"He was Greyson Isador," Alrik said softly.

"Her brother?"

He shook his head. "Her Blood. We take our queen's house name. I don't know what accommodations she made for her Blood when she left the nest, but he went rogue and became a thrall. I don't think he meant to kill her at all. He was just desperate to feed from his queen, who unfortunately, was no longer queen and had no power to share."

I looked up at him. "So you're Alrik and Daire Isador now?"

"Yes." Pride surged through the bond from both of them. Pride at belonging to me.

A silver sedan drove down the road and parked next to their motorcycles. Evidently it was time to meet Ms. Talbott. I don't know why I was so nervous, but I had to scrub my sweaty palms on my jeans as we walked back. I reached for Alrik's hand, but noticed something odd. Now that someone else was here, Daire walked in front of me, and Alrik walked slightly behind. He did take my hand, but stayed behind me, rather than walking alongside as he'd done before.

:*Protection,*: he murmured through the bond. :*I have your back. Daire has your front. None shall threaten you, my queen. Not even your consiliarius, if that's who she is.*:

Ms. Talbott was an ageless, elegant beauty with gleaming ebony skin. I had no idea of her exact age, but she had the impact and weight of a mature woman used to kicking ass and taking names. She wore eggplant-colored trousers and a tweedy long jacket with a belt that made me think British, though I had no idea, really. She hadn't sounded British on the phone. As we neared, she fucking curtsied, right there in the street, and kept her head bowed.

"Forgive me, Your Majesty. I failed you, and I failed your dear mother."

"Please, don't. It's not your fault Mom was killed." It made me uncomfortable to see her bowing like that, begging for forgiveness. I didn't even know the woman. But I could tell through the bond that her apology made Alrik look more favorably on her. Maybe this was all for show, just to convince him that she could be trusted.

"But it is my fault that you were lost for so long." Straightening, she looked at me, her eyes swimming with tears. "How have you survived?"

I shrugged, not willing to go into details with someone I didn't know. "Luck, mostly."

"I have a feeling it was quite a bit more than luck, Your Majesty. But let's get you safely inside. I have much to share with you." She unlocked the truck of her car. A white blanket embroidered with gold and silver covered something rectangular. She lifted the whole thing, leaving the blanket on, and offered it to me. "If one of the Blood can carry the legacy, I'll open the gate and unlock the house."

This was what all the fuss was about? Something small enough that she could easily lift it? The cloth-draped box was only two-foot long and only a foot or so deep. I gave a little mental signal to Daire and he took the item from her arms, holding it as reverently as if it was a newborn infant.

Ms. Talbott unlocked the gate and we walked up the sidewalk to the grand entry. "The estate has been kept exactly as your mother ordered, ready for the moment I could locate you. Water, electricity, everything is on and ready for your use. A housekeeper comes in once a week and keeps the refrigerator and pantry stocked."

She pushed the heavy door open and stepped back, waiting for me to pass through. I stared up at the stained glass transom above the old oak door, remembering. I used to sit on the floor in the entryway, covered in prisms and drops of colored light from the window. I thought that window was magical, even though it was only bevels and colored bits of glass. I glanced down and a clean line of salt had been poured across the doorway. The same as Mom had taught me from the beginning.

Safe—or as safe as I'd ever been in my life.

I stepped inside, waiting to feel... something. Maybe the underlying tension I'd never been able to shake since I'd gone on the run would ease. Maybe I'd feel peace, real peace. But no, I was still fully aware of the monsters outside. The salt and iron would certainly deter them, but nothing would keep them out for long.

:Nothing but us, my queen." Alrik said in my head. *"This isn't your nest. It wasn't even Selena's nest. Just as safe as she could make it without power.:*

Which meant without blood. I understood that much now.

I LED them into the front sitting room and pulled the curtains open so that sunlight would come in through the large window. An original four-sided fireplace dominated the heart of the home, lending heat to the sitting room, dining room, kitchen, and office on the main floor. To my knowledge, it still worked, though I don't remember Mom ever using it. The same furniture faced the hearth: two wingback chairs at one end, with two leather loveseats on either side. I don't know why Mom felt the need for so many seats—I couldn't remember ever having guests. But maybe she'd remembered having many Blood and guests in her nest, wherever that had been.

:London,: Daire sent me through our bond.

That made sense. She'd told me several stories about life in London, though she'd never sounded nostalgic.

The wingback chairs looked more throne-like, which was maybe why I instinctively avoided them and went to the leather sofa. Of course that also allowed my men to sit on either side of me. Daire set the covered box down on the coffee table and Ms. Talbott stood beside it, her hands clasped in front of her.

"The night of your mother's death, she called my office and left a message for me," she began. "Unfortunately, she didn't call my direct number. To this day, I don't know why. She had it. She could have called me for assistance at any time of the day or night, same as you. By leaving the message on the office line, my arrival was delayed until 8:15 AM the next day, and you were already gone. I immediately contacted the authorities to report your absence and your mother's murder, which the police decided had been done by a pack of wild dogs. I didn't try to conceal her death in anyway, so as to give the police urgency, and they did search for you for months. But you must have been long gone before I managed to get word to the authorities."

"I left at dawn," I answered softly, not wanting to remember that terror. I'd never been alone before and my mother had just been slaughtered. "I walked down the street to the bus stop at the park. I'd seen people getting off and on it for years. I asked the driver to take me as far away from home as he could and then he dropped me off at the Greyhound ticket office. I didn't know where to go, I just knew I needed to get away as fast as possible. So I took the next bus out of state. It just happened to be headed to Memphis."

"Why didn't you stay in the house, wait for help?"

My stomach churned. Alrik pressed tighter to my side and dropped his arm over my shoulders, hugging me closer. "The one who killed Mom knew I was watching. He came as close to the house as he could, even reached through the fence toward me, and he said he'd be back. He'd wait every night until I came to him. I'd never be free of him."

"I'll fucking cut the bastard's head off as soon as he dares come within a mile of you," Daire retorted. His voice vibrated with the deeper growl of his warcat.

"So I ran," I whispered, reaching out to squeeze Daire's hand and keep him beside me. The thought of losing him made my stomach heave. I'd seen that monster kill the two most important people in my life and survived... but I didn't think I'd survive either his or Alrik's death.

:Nothing will take us from you.: Daire prowled in my mind, sinuous fur winding through me. *:Not even death.:*

"What did you do for money?" Ms. Talbott asked, dabbing at her eyes with a tissue.

"Mom had a stash of coins and money in a lock box under her bed. I used that until I could get a job."

She shuddered delicately as if she'd bitten into something nasty. "Goddess. That was never supposed to happen. Let's start at the beginning, shall we? I'm sure your Blood have explained some of our ways, but I'll assume you know nothing, and always, please, I beg you, ask. I am fully at your service."

Daire made a rude noise of aggravation that made her smile. "Not that kind of service. I'm not enough Aima to serve in that capacity, but closer to you than a full human. My grandmother once tracked back twenty generations and found where her mother left her queen's nest and married a commoner. As they had children, and grandchildren, the Aima blood thinned, though enough remains in my family today that I'm able to serve as consiliarius to Isador, as my mother and her grandmother before. Though I doubt I'll live quite as long as Grandmama, who served as consiliarius up to her one-hundredth birthday and lived over a decade longer telling my mother everything she was doing wrong."

She smiled, pausing a moment. "As consiliarius, I'm your counsel in all things legal, whether human or Aima courts. I know the world's laws, and I know Triune law. I've studied them all my life, though I haven't personally met any of the high queens."

"Few have," Alrik added, "At least outside their own Blood and consiliari."

"Who or what is the Triune?" I asked.

"The Triune is composed of the highest and most powerful queens who can track their bloodlines directly back to the great goddesses. We used to have a Triune of Triune—three seats on three courts—but over the centuries we've lost too many royals houses to keep all nine seats open. Generally, when we refer to Triune, we mean any of the high queens, unless they specify one court or the other. The eldest is Marne Ceresa and legend says even she doesn't remember how old she is any longer, but we conservatively acknowledge that she's at least one thousand years old. Queens generally become more powerful as they age, so the eldest queens currently hold the Triune seats."

"So I probably won't ever see one of these Triune queens?"

She grimaced and shrugged her shoulders. "I wouldn't go so far as to say that, Your Majesty. If a Triune summons any other Aima, queen or not, they go. At once. The last few centuries, Aima power has waned. Greatly. Queens have been lost, like you, disappearing into the masses of humanity. We lost the third court entirely, and now the Aima Triune is down to only two seats. The queens that remain fight viciously for that third seat, and though you're extremely young, you're also extremely powerful. You will be viewed as a direct threat for that third seat."

"I hate politics! The last thing I'd want to do is fight for a seat on the Triune. Besides, Dad was human. Surely they wouldn't want a half-human queen on the Triune."

Alrik squeezed my shoulders, but Daire's eyes were bright, his warcat eager to jump into the fray. Evidently he thought fighting for a seat on the Triune would be great fun.

"You may not have a choice," she continued, her face solemn. "It doesn't matter what you say, but only what the other queens believe. Isis is one of the greatest goddesses and her gifts are fearsome indeed. You will have few friends on the mid-tier courts, I'm afraid."

"Which is why we need to establish her nest," Alrik said. "And we need more Blood. We have to stake her claim and keep her safe from anyone who thinks they can eliminate the upstart American queen with an eye on the Triune."

"I can definitely help you with securing a nest, whether you want to remain here or not," Ms. Talbott said. "I agree your nest is our first priority, but I can also counsel you on all things political and strategical. You may, of course, replace me with any counsel of your own choosing at any time. Tradition has kept Talbotts serving Isador for many generations, but we serve at the queen's discretion."

"Were you with Mom in London?"

"I was."

She didn't offer any other information, but looked at me steadily. Open to my questions—but also reserved. She didn't know me, either. Or maybe that reservation was built from generations of holding these secrets close. "No offense, but I don't remember you."

"The geas upon your mother affected me indirectly, because I know all the secrets of the Aima court. Selena was able to discuss general things with me, to a point, but not your ascension or the legacy, at least directly. We had an agreement that I would be allowed to sit down with you and begin your transition after you turned eighteen. Unfortunately, she was killed, and you disappeared before I could make contact."

"Have you had any contact with the other conciliari?" Alrik asked.

She shook her head. "Once Selena left the court, all contact was broken. I maintained the estate and legacy finances for her, but I never communicated Shara's birth or disappearance, for that matter."

"That seems... odd." I sensed suspicion and distrust in Alrik's bond. It made me feel better to know I wasn't the only one sitting here with doubts about this woman's loyalty. "A new Isador queen was born, completely out of a nest with no protection whatsoever, and you never contacted anyone, even a Triune consiliarius, to ask for assistance or forbearance for Selena's heir?"

Ms. Talbott stared down at her hands, tightly clenched in her lap. "I tried. On your sweet life, Shara, I tried, but I didn't even know of your existence until you were almost a year old. She refused to allow one peep of your existence to spread. She refused to send you to another queen's nest. She refused to send for any assistance of any kind. I thought perhaps that after your father died that she would return to the fold, and take you to safety, but if anything, she became more erratic and paranoid."

"She said they would want me dead," I said softly, watching her reaction.

Ms. Talbott raised her head, her eyes hard. "They may try, but they'll find this consiliarius very difficult to work around."

Daire let out a huff. "We're her Blood. Her safety is our concern."

"Your physical strength and proximity are indeed her best defense. But there are ways I can protect that wouldn't occur to a Blood. Money can open—or close—many doors that your impressive muscles won't budge. Don't you think they tried to find Selena even though she left the London nest? Many wanted her dead because she betrayed her house and court. They couldn't understand why she'd turn her back on such power and prestige, so they distrusted her motivations. I created such a complex tangle of shell cooperations and false identities that even Ceresa's consiliarius couldn't find us in over thirty years."

I'd had no idea. All those years, I'd never known this woman existed, yet she'd been working to keep Mom, and me, ultimately, hidden from some very powerful people. I still didn't know if I could trust—

A resonate ting sounded in my head, as if someone had tapped a crystal that hummed and vibrated. It sounded pure and vibrant. A message from the goddess? Some element of my power? I wasn't sure, but I knew what it meant. Gina Talbott was worth my trust.

"Where do we start?" I asked.

Her shoulders relaxed slightly, the only outward sign of her relief, but inside, she was nearly sobbing with relief. I could sense it.

"The legacy. You must make formal claim."

She leaned forward and pulled the cloth away from the object we'd brought from her car. A wooden box sat on the coffee table with a single symbol carved on each side, dark and rich with age. I wouldn't have recognized it before, only that it was Egyptian, but after tasting the goddess's blood, I knew that symbol as the tyet, knot of Isis. Inlaid in the top was a mosaic pattern of Isis, easily recognizable with her disk and horned crown, the same as in my vision. One of her arms pointed up, with a golden bowl in her hand. The box had no visible padlock or edges. It didn't look like it opened at all.

"No one can open this box but a direct descendant of Isis. Only house Isador remains after thousands of years, and only you remain of house Isador. There are stories of sister-queens fighting to the death for the chance to open the box." She smiled faintly. "Though I don't know that such tales are true, or if they were spread by the other houses jealous of Isis's legacy."

"What is the legacy? I guess I thought it was just an inheritance, whatever money you've managed for Mom."

"It is, but it's so much more too. Some of it you may never understand, let alone use, but it's your birthright. Know that many have died trying to possess Isis's legacy, and there will be people who will try to use you, in order to wield the legacy for themselves."

"In other words, trust no one." Alrik's said in an iron voice.

"But us, of course," Daire added.

Ms. Talbott looked steadily at me. "And me."

"The four musketeers." Letting a grin spread, I nodded, acknowledging each of them. "You said more Blood will come. How am I to know which ones to trust?"

"Blood will come to your call, yes." Alrik tightened his arm around my shoulders and I felt a heaviness in his bond. Hesitation, though honest. "But not all Blood..."

He blew out a sigh and looked at Daire for help.

"Not all Blood are as perfect as us?"

Ms. Talbott choked back a laugh. "Well, I'm sure you're perfectly delightful Blood in every way, but I think what he's trying to say is that not all Blood will come because they love you. Or because they honestly want to protect you. Some will come for power. Others will come because their current queen ordered them to."

My eyes widened. "Wait, what? Like spies? For other queens?"

She tipped her head. "It's very common at court, certainly. Every queen has eyes and ears on the others."

Now I felt stupid. Really stupid. I thought Alrik and Daire had come to me to love and protect me. That all who came would be like them. We'd make love and feed each other, laugh and play games and go places...

Alrik cupped my cheek, turning my face to him. "We shall

86

do all those things and more, my queen. And the Blood you want to keep will also love you. It's not a stupid or naive thought at all."

"If a Blood comes that I don't like, or doesn't feel right, do I have to accept him?"

"Not just males. There are female and non-gendered Blood. And no, you don't. If another queen is sending the Blood as a gift, then there will be consequences if you refuse, but you're not obligated to share your blood with anyone but whom you choose."

I hadn't been doing this for long, but already, I knew one thing. Power rose in me, lending weight to my words. "I won't take a Blood that I don't love, and who doesn't love me. I won't give someone I don't trust access to my mind and heart and power. I don't care who that ticks off. I won't do it."

Both Alrik and Daire ducked their heads. "As my queen orders, so it shall be."

"Take the legacy," Ms. Talbott said softly, drawing my attention back to her. "Claim what's yours, Your Majesty."

12

ALRIK

Hearing my queen say that she wouldn't take a Blood that she didn't love was an unexpected, glorious boon from Isis herself.

After years of serving as a minor sib, I was eager for power, yes. I was eager for royal blood. Hot for the queen's body. Fuck yeah.

Then Shara called me in the night and I wanted her, and her alone. For all time. It was just... right. I had no doubts or hesitations in coming to her side. I'd do whatever I had to do to keep her safe. Kill. Lie. Cheat. Steal.

Make love to her, and her other Blood, however she wished. I could not fucking wait.

Few Blood were as lucky as Daire and I right now. Blood might be bonded to a queen, and they had the power given to them by her blood, sure. Maybe even semi-regular fucking. But a powerful queen had many Blood to entertain her. The jostling and planning and backstabbing to get to the queen's bed could be more brutal than a gladiator's fight.

Of course the alternative was just as unattractive. No one wanted to serve a weak queen who had few Blood, even if that meant they had easy access to her blood and bed. Weak queens were absorbed into larger nests, and became queen-sibs to the more powerful queens. We had another name for that kind of queen.

Pawn.

So the chances that a queen would actually love her Blood...

A motherfucking rarity.

Shara looked at the box and gnawed on her bottom lip. My dick went rock hard. "How do I claim the legacy?"

Ms. Talbott pointed to the upturned hand of the goddess engraved on the box. "Press your thumb into the cup she's holding, and make your offering."

The cup was made from a slightly rounded golden disk, with a tiny spike at the center that wasn't noticeable if you didn't know to look for it. Shara did as she asked, a soft sigh escaping her lips at the prick to her thumb. Instantly, I smelled her blood. My mouth watered, and Daire made a low, rumbling purr of hunger.

"Steady, boys," Ms. Talbott laughed, shaking her head.

Shara's scent rose higher, blood and sex and moonlit pools, sparkling sands and flowering jasmine. I quivered, fighting the urge to haul her against me and bury my fangs in her throat. Or better yet, beg her to test whether her fangs had come in yet on me.

The box clicked and an edge appeared all around the top. A hush fell in the room, so quiet I could hear her heart beating.

With trembling hands, she reached out and removed the top of the box. All three of us leaned closer to get a better look.

The inside of the box was lined in carnelian, painstakingly cut into thin, flat pieces. Four cannisters sat inside the box, each carved with a different lid.

"Are they... burial jars? I can't think what the name is," Shara said.

"Canopic jars, and no, they're not," Ms. Talbott answered. "Those came to represent the four sons of Horus. These are unique. If you showed them to a Egyptologist, he'd say they were fakes despite their obvious age. They have the wrong lids. Some say these represent Her four daughters, though you probably won't find much about them except for Bastet and Ammit."

Shara stretched out her index finger but didn't actually touch the beautifully carved cat on top of the nearest jar. Another bore a hooded cobra with impossibly long pointed fangs. "Not Her daughters. They're pieces of Herself. Her... gifts."

"These are the truths revealed by the blood of the goddess that runs in your veins."

Shara leaned back against me and shivered slightly, so I wrapped my arm around her, pulling her into my warmth. "What do I do with them?"

"You need do nothing with them. The power associated with Isis's gifts is already yours to command. These are merely representations, or maybe talismans would be a better word. This is your legacy, passed down through thousands of years. She's here in these jars, because She is in you. She *is* you. In your case, wholly you, because She has no other heirs left."

"I'm not her. I'm not... a goddess."

"Yes, you are," I said firmly, pressing my lips to Shara's head. "You're She. Isis incarnate."

"I'm Shara," she said firmly, burrowing tighter into my embrace.

"Yes," I whispered, breathing in my scent. "Shara. Isador. Last living daughter of Isis. Last to carry Her blood on this earth. In that regard, you are Isis."

"And that's why they will want you dead." Ms. Talbott picked up the lid of the box, holding it out to Shara. An old leather book was strapped inside. "Your family history, plus some surprises your ancestors left behind. Just in case. It's a sort of Isador Book of Shadows."

Shara unbuckled the leather straps holding the book in place and took it. "Have you read it?"

"Absolutely not. I'd probably catch on fire if I tried to touch any of it. Though I have seen the legacy opened twice."

"Mom and…?"

"Her sister." Ms. Talbott placed the lid back on the box and covered it. Then she opened up her briefcase and pulled out a thick manila folder. "Now, let's go over a few things—"

"I have an aunt?"

Her mouth tightened and she shook her head. "No. It's complicated. Selena's sister is no more."

Shara stared at her a moment. "You can't say her name."

Ms. Talbott gave her a small, sad smile and inclined her head. "Your Majesty, if we may proceed, I'd like to show you the rest of your legacy. This side, financial. As you can see, you're an extremely wealthy young woman."

Shara turned her head to me. "Do you know who my aunt was?"

I shook my head. "Sorry, no, I never heard that tale. Daire, do you know?"

"Nope."

I could feel her curiosity burning in our bond. Curiosity that might get her into trouble… or worse, hurt. "If Ms. Talbott is under a geas not to say your aunt's name, or tell anyone about her, then you must ask yourself who would do such a thing? Who would want her silenced?"

"The Triune," she whispered. "But why? First, Mom abandons everything she knows, including her power, and lives like a human. And now I hear I have an aunt that Mom never mentioned. What am I getting myself into here?"

"Aima court games." Daire said. "It's like a snake's den, crocodile watering hole, and cock fight all at the same time."

"Sounds terrible."

"It is," Ms. Talbott agreed. "And please, call me Gina. That's one of the greatest benefits to being so far from court. We can just be ourselves. There's no strict rules of procession and titles that we must go by."

"So says the woman who curtsied and called me 'Your Majesty.'"

Gina laughed. "Guilty as charged. Now please, Shara," she said with emphasis, "take a look at your accounts. Everything's in order."

Shara glanced at the top paper and shuffled through several pages. Froze. Then went back to the first page. "Really? That's what I'm worth? Is that even a real number?"

"Indeed it is. The Isador legacy is massive. It's been accumulating for thousands of years, expanding and changing over the years. I've worked with my team to keep your investments well diversified, mostly conservative, and you're still worth more than the Queen of England and Bill Gates put together."

Which pissed me off all over again. "Shara should have been wrapped in luxury her entire life, rather than starving, homeless, and scared."

"I know." Gina leaned forward and reached out to touch Shara's knee. "I hate that so many things went wrong. I hate that I wasn't able to help you when you needed help the most. And if there's anything I can do now, no matter how small, that's my job, and my pleasure. I live to serve you and house Isador."

Shara placed her hand over Gina's and smiled. "It's not your fault that I had no idea all this existed. Thanks for taking care of everything for so long." She looked at me and Daire, her face softening. "I know it makes you angry, but I'm sort of glad I had these past years alone. It was awful at times—but I also learned how to be on my own, how to protect myself, and how to live in the real world with very few resources or help. I have a feeling I'm going to need all those skills and more to deal with the Triune."

Gina spent the next hour going over bank and credit cards, how to access her money at any time with a phone call, and then made arrangements to get her passport picture taken. "Can you drive? Or do you have the desire to learn?"

"I took driver's ed in school before I left, but I never got my license. I could use a refresher."

"Your mother's car is in the garage. I'll arrange a private instructor." Gina laid out a set of keys. "These are spares, in case you can't find hers. We've had it serviced regularly and the tank is full. Will you be living here?"

She looked around the room and then settled her gaze on me. "What do you think?"

"Daire and I will explore the exterior, see how defensible the house is. I saw the salt walking in, but that doesn't mean the whole house is safe." I listened to her bond, sorting through her emotions. She was a bit numb from all the bombshells and exhausted. Rest would be ideal before she had to make any decisions. Deeper, though, I sensed sadness, and even fear. No matter how safe we made this house, she'd always remember her parents had died here. I didn't think she'd want to make this place her permanent nest. "Daire, why don't you start the inspection. I'll make some dinner. Gina, will you stay?"

"Thank you, but no." Gina stood, so Shara did too, and I stood with my queen. "I'm sure you're exhausted and you need time to sort things through without a stranger to interfere. My card is in the folder, and..." She set a cell phone on the table and then snapped her briefcase closed. "My number is already programmed in. Call me day or night. It doesn't matter how minor the question or need, Your Majesty. I'm at your disposal."

Shara hugged her. Surprise flickered over Gina's face, then teary affection and gratitude. "Thank you for everything."

Gina sniffed as she pulled back and gathered her things. "No, thank you, Shara. I'm so honored to work for you. I'll leave the legacy with you for now, but it doesn't have to stay in your presence to give you power. I thought you might like to have access to it for a few days."

Shara glanced at the four jars warily, as if they might come alive and bite her. "Are they safe to touch and handle?"

"Of course. They've survived thousands of years, dozens of

wars, and even queen fighting queen to possess. I doubt you could break one of the jars if you tried. But when you're finished with them, I'll put them back in the safe. I also have a large amount of Isador jewelry stored for you. When you want to examine or take any of it, please let me know."

"Should I hide it somewhere in the house?" Shara put the lid back on the box and the lines disappeared, making it look like one seamless block of wood again. "I don't think we have a safe here. I guess I could lock it in the safe room."

"You don't feel it, since the legacy is yours." Gina covered the box with the white blanket, tucking it over the old book on the coffee table. "But I've been told there's an overwhelming sense of dread and danger that anyone else feels when they come close to it. For someone to mess with it, they'd have to get through the locked gates and doors, bypass your Blood, and then overcome the legacy's own protections to take it. Even if they took it, they wouldn't be able to open it. So I see no reason you can't just leave it here until you're ready for me to return it to the safe with your jewels."

We saw her out, and after I shut and locked the front door, she stood in the entry way, looking a little lost. She hugged herself, looking around as if she'd never seen the house before, yet recognized every room. I took her hand and kissed her knuckles. I smelled a hint of blood, and so turned her hand until I found her thumb that she'd pricked to open the legacy. I licked the dried smear from her skin, and even that small taste made hunger twist like a knife in my stomach.

She stepped closer, linking her arms around my neck, and laid her head on my chest. I held her, giving her all my strength and comfort through the bond.

"It's... weird. To be here, I mean, in my parents home, without them. There's a lot of memories here, both good and bad. But mostly bad. It's easy to forget all the good times, you know?"

"Yeah." I tightened my arms, determined to wipe the many

years of fear and loneliness from her memory. "So let's work hard on creating some new good memories."

DAIRE

EVEN IN BROAD DAYLIGHT, my cat prowled beneath the surface. I could almost feel its fur beneath my skin, rolling and swishing like a tail.

I paced the exterior of the house, checking all windows and access points. Ms. Talbott's crew knew what they were about. A thick line of salt encircled the entire house in safety. The windows were all original leaded glass, full of minerals and impurities that thralls wouldn't easily break through. A solid wrought iron fence surrounded the yard, with tight, locked gates.

I accidentally stepped on one of the border plants, and smelled garlic. An usual planting for sure, but another deterrent. Thorny rose bushes added to the defenses.

Solid brick, wrought iron, salt. Not impenetrable, but definitely difficult for one of the thralls to get through without causing itself damage.

I paused, looking up at the house. It had that old-world mansion feel, but somehow I couldn't see Shara here. I'd be surprised if she wanted to make a nest here, but the choice was hers. I'd live in an off-grid hut in Alaska as long as she was there.

I was tempted to open a vein and line the property with my blood as an extra warning. But I didn't want to waste my blood if she wanted it. She hadn't fed today.

I didn't need to search for her bond. She glowed like moonfire in my mind, spinning rainbows and light into the darkest corners. She didn't like being back in the house much. So I definitely wasn't going to mark the entire property with my blood.

Hurrying back to her side, I found them in the kitchen. She

sat on the center island watching Rik at the stove. She looked so fucking adorable, swinging her legs, still in her leather jacket that she'd been so excited to get. Fucking made me want to buy her something every single day just to see her smile like that again.

That was better than beating the shit out of no one in particular to get the rage out of my head that she'd been denied so much for most of her life. The welcoming smile on her lips pulled me in like a ceaseless tide. I wrapped an arm around her and tucked my nose against her throat.

"Smells good," and I didn't mean just the food.

"Alrik said he's never seen a better-stocked refrigerator. It looks like a grocery store in here. A high-end crazy grocery store. It's a good thing he didn't ask me what I wanted him to make because I wouldn't have any idea."

I didn't meet Rik's gaze for fear that both of us would spontaneously combust with fury. I didn't want to think about the nights she hadn't had enough to eat. Or the fact that she didn't have more than a single backpack of possessions. "Whatever he makes will be good, I promise you that."

"Good, but not spectacular." Rik scraped diced vegetables into the pan. "I'm not a chef, but I'm a passable cook. We need to start taking you to all the five-star restaurants in the country. That would be fun."

Her mouth turned down. "Sounds too fancy."

For me. Though she didn't say it, I saw it in the way she ducked her head. I glanced at Rik and a muscle in his jaw ticked. "Nonsense. That would give us an excuse to do lots of shopping too. Not just leather jackets, either. Though if you want one in every color of the rainbow, I'm sure that can be accomplished."

She heaved out a huge sigh, as if I'd told her we were dragging her to the dentist every day for a month. "I don't need much. Really. I don't place value on possessions, or fancy clothes. I have simple wants. And I certainly don't want a bunch of crap slowing us down if we have to make a run for it."

"You have a rock troll and a warcat at your side now." Alrik tossed the sauteed vegetables with cooked pasta, added freshly grated Parmesan cheese, and swirled with a little olive oil to finish. "We don't make a run for it. We stake your territory and then we bleed to keep it."

I hit the wine fridge and pulled out a nice Pinot Grigio. I wasn't sure of my queen's tastes yet, but a crisp blanc would go well with the pasta.

We ate in the breakfast nook in the large kitchen rather than carrying everything to the formal dining room. The housekeeper definitely deserved a raise, even if Ms. Talbott was already paying her handsomely. The wine was fantastic and Rik had managed to find a crusty Italian bread too.

"This is a feast," Shara said around a mouthful of pasta. "I can't believe you threw this together in just a few minutes."

"Simple but good food doesn't need a lot of ingredients, but I'm afraid I don't know a ton of dishes. You'll get tired of pasta pretty quickly."

"I can grill steaks, chicken, that kind of thing," I added. "Plus we both can make pancakes and eggs, though my specialty is grilled cheese sandwiches."

"Sounds good to me, and I want you to teach me so I can contribute."

I wanted to protest that there was no need for her to cook, but she meant well. She wanted to do her part, and certainly didn't want us to feel as though we had to wait on her hand and foot.

When that's exactly what we *wanted* to do.

"We should also ask Ms. Talbott to find us a personal chef," Rik said. "Especially as more and more Blood come to your call. It'll eventually be difficult to keep us all fed without help."

She buttered a piece of bread and nibbled on the crunchy

crust before answering. "I don't really want us to get that... big. I like it just being us."

"Which I love, don't get me wrong, but you need more than two Blood. Both for defense against thralls, and the other queens. It's a cutthroat court."

"But if I don't go to court, why would I ever even see any other queens?"

"Daire's better at understanding court etiquette than I am. Can you explain?"

I refilled our glasses and leaned back in the chair. "It's like politics." She made a sound of disgust that made me smirk. "Every queen has her own court, and yes, there's jostling for position. The larger her court, the more her power and protection. But the larger her court, the more her Blood and sibs will struggle to gain her attention. All power trickles down from the queen, and naturally, those on the bottom want and need more."

"We already talked about this. I said I didn't want a Blood I don't love and trust, and I don't want a huge court of people I barely know."

I took another sip of wine, trying to find the best way to explain. Then I decided to just lay it out on the line. "If you only have two Blood, we'll love you and you'll love us, and then we'll die. Because we weren't strong enough to hold your position."

She gasped and Rik shot me a dark look. "He's exaggerating."

"No, I'm not. You and I both know it. How many American queens are there? Name them."

"Our former queen, Keisha Skye in New York City."

I held up one finger, waiting. I knew he'd have a hard time coming up with any others. America wasn't known for queens for a very particular reason.

"Leonie. In New Orleans."

"That's two."

"There's one in Texas, I think. But I don't remember her name."

"Even if I give that one to you, I bet you can't name a fourth."

Rik didn't like losing, even to me. "What's your point?"

"America is still a young country compared to Isis's kingdom. Most American queens are younger than the queens of the Old World, and thus, weaker. They don't last long without allying with older, stronger queens. Keisha became Rosalind's lover for that reason, though they'll both argue the other is her queen-sib. Everyone leaves Leonie alone because it's New Orleans and vampires are good for business, but last I heard, the Texas queen had fled back to Mexico."

"If she has enough Blood…"

I leaned toward him, challenging him with a direct stare. He bristled, as any alpha would, but I wanted him to fight. For me, for her, for us. "Why did you want to leave New York City and look for our own queen, against all hope?"

"You know why."

I tipped my head toward Shara without breaking eye contact with him. "*She* doesn't."

He stared at me, eyes narrowed, and I tensed, braced for war. No alpha appreciated a blatant challenge—especially in front of his mate and queen. His shoulders squared, his chest and arms bulging as he instinctively tried to intimidate me into backing down. Even when she looked back and forth between us, her brow furrowed with worry.

"Because," he finally sighed and allowed his shoulders to relax. "There have been rumors."

I slowly exhaled, relieved that he'd conceded. I'd rather use our energy to please our queen than beat the shit out of each other. "Rumors that some lesser queens have gone into hiding in order to stay under the Triune's radar, and America is great for hiding. We were *allowed* to roam around the countryside and see if we could find anyone in need of protection."

"And you found me," Shara said. "Wait, allowed? By who?"

Ah, my queen did not like the thought that another had commanded us. "Our queen at the time. Keisha Skye."

"The New York queen."

I nodded. "She allowed us to leave with the hope that we'd find a harried, scared minor queen and bring her back into the fold. *Her* fold, naturally. We wanted to leave to find our own queen, and if she was strong enough, never return. No one expected us to find a lost Isador heir who could someday rival even Marne Ceresa in power."

Her eyes widened. "I'm that strong? Or will be?"

"Absolutely. If you take more Blood. If you allow them to take sibs under you. Even better if someone like Leonie would consider becoming your ally." I held Shara's gaze, letting her see the truth in my words and the decades of court experience I'd honed. I'd known from the beginning I would never be an alpha. I needed other ways to protect my queen, if I ever was so lucky to find one, and so dedicated myself to court politics. "If you do nothing, you'll be absorbed into another more powerful queen's territory."

"Or killed," Rik said reluctantly. "All of us."

13

SHARA

reat. Just great. The more I learned about the Triune and the other queens, the less I wanted to be a part of it. Which made sense. My own mother had given up her power and fled court to live in exile.

"You don't have to make any decisions right now," Alrik said, reaching over to lightly touch my arm. "It's impossible to know at this point. We have no idea how many Blood will come to you, or how many lost or rogue queens may be secreted away. Goddess knows we had no idea we'd find you in Arkansas of all places."

"It's just…" I struggled to find the words to say what I was feeling.

"It's a roller coaster." For once, Daire seemed somber, his eyes dark and solemn rather than dancing with amusement or mischief. "You were alone. Then we found you. And your whole world changed."

"Yeah." I blew out a sigh. "Don't get me wrong—I wouldn't change it for the world."

"We blew your mind last night."

There was his wicked smirk, and yeah, they had totally

blown my mind. Remembering made my inner muscles clench. "Maybe I should blow your minds tonight."

Alrik pushed his chair away from the table, evidently taking that as a signal that we should begin right away. Not that I had a problem with that. At all. Though I didn't stand, even as Daire joined his friend. They stood, alert, eager, yet also… compliant. It was so strange. I had no idea that two such heavily muscled, powerful, strong attractive men could be so… so…

I couldn't even think of the word. Submissive wasn't the right word. They did wait for my command, but it wasn't like they *needed* my command. They were just patiently waiting for me to decide when and how.

"Or for you to signal to one of us that we should take over." Alrik's voice had gone smoky and low, making my nipples harden.

I picked up my wine glass and stood, slowly, enjoying the way they watched me. "Can someone grab the bottle? I've never had wine before and I like it."

Alrik grabbed the bottle before Daire could, so he grabbed the men's glasses and stepped back into the kitchen to get another bottle. "Anything else, my queen? Chocolates? Strawberries? I think I saw some fresh ones in the fridge."

"Maybe later."

They both watched me, eyes growing heavy with desire. It made me put a little sway in my steps as I headed for the stairs. I glanced back over my shoulder, waiting for Alrik to look up from my ass and catch my gaze. It took him several long moments. "My queen?"

"Is it safe here?"

"Of course. We wouldn't stay here at all if I felt you might be in danger."

Daire stepped closer to him, pressing against his side. He draped an arm across his shoulders and whispered—but pitched so his voice would carry to me. "She means is it safe enough for us both in her bed."

I wouldn't have thought it possible, but Alrik's eyes smoldered even hotter. He reached around Daire's head and fisted his hand in his hair, pulling his head back a little, baring his throat. While he kept his eyes locked on me. "I'll have to see the bedroom first. See how secure it is. And then our queen can feast on your blood while I fuck you."

OH. MY. Hot chills raced through me, making me quiver. I should have turned around and led the way as quickly as possible to my room, but looking at them, I couldn't move.

Alrik came up the stairs and lifted me against him, somehow without sloshing a single drop of wine out of my glass. I wrapped my legs around his waist and pressed my lips to his throat. His pulse pounded beneath his skin and he smelled so good. Hot stone, a hint of smoke, all that power and fury. I wanted to feast on him. On Daire. On them both.

I bit his throat and he let out a rumbling growl of encouragement, but I couldn't do it. I pressed harder, I envisioned my fangs coming out, sinking into him, and I wanted it. I wanted to penetrate him with my own teeth and taste that first hot salty surge of his blood on my tongue. But my damned human genes wouldn't let it happen. At least not yet. I made a frustrated sound half way between a growl and a wail.

And Daire was suddenly there. He actually knocked Alrik sideways into the wall with the force of his attack. A bottle of wine went rolling down the stairs. Hopefully that was the one we hadn't opened yet. I smelled blood. Daire bit him higher, just beneath his ear, and let the blood trail down his throat to me. Sweeter than the wine, better than the food, better than anything I'd ever tasted before. The wound was bigger too, as if he'd torn open Alrik's throat. So much blood. Surely that wasn't good for him to lose so much blood…

"We're Blood. This is what we live for." Alrik shifted me higher against him. "Daire, go find us a bed."

Daire licked up what I missed, swiping his tongue across the edge of my mouth and Alrik's skin, but then he backed away.

Through the bond, I said, :*Not my parent's bed.*:

"Which was your old room?"

I closed my eyes, clamping my mouth tighter to Alrik's throat. My head buzzed as if I'd thrown back half a dozen shots, but I couldn't get enough of his blood. I didn't want to lift my mouth and waste a single drop. :*Second door on the right, up the next flight of stairs.*:

Daire raced ahead, scouting the way, and I felt the moment he entered my old room. Because a dark wall of rage hit me through the bond.

In a few moments, Alrik entered the room I'd grown up in. It was pitch black, but evidently they didn't need light to see. There wasn't much to see anyway. Just four walls, the door, and the bed.

I felt the need to try and explain. "It was the only room in the house that didn't have windows."

"This is a prison cell." Daire growled, his voice so feral I could barely understand his words. "Not a bedroom. Especially for a child. Let alone a queen."

"When I was little and Dad was still alive, I slept with them," I whispered. "Mom said I never slept well alone. I would cry and fuss until she held me. She had no idea why, until she saw a monster trying to break through the window, tapping on the glass. After Dad died, I slept with her awhile, but as I got older, I really wanted my own space. I actually liked it up here. I called it my tower. The hatch in the roof made me feel like I could escape if I needed to, though I don't know how I would have gotten off the roof without breaking a leg."

Alrik leaned down and set me carefully on the bed. He didn't straighten, but looked me squarely in the eyes. "This is not going to be your nest. We will find a place where our queen may have as many windows as she likes and still feel safe."

"Deal." I tried to hold his gaze, but he still bled. It stained his t-shirt, wet cotton sticking to his ripped muscles. Reminding me of the way his body had moved against mine last night. How much strength rolled through that big body of his. "So is this safe enough for me to have you both?"

He pressed his mouth to mine, stroking his tongue between my lips. Tasting his blood on my tongue. I forgot I still held my wine glass, until I felt Daire take it from my hand. He set the other glasses and the opened wine bottle on the nightstand beside the bed. Against my lips, Alrik whispered, "How do you want us?"

I pushed my tongue into his mouth, tasting the wine. Wondering what my blood would taste like on his tongue. "I want what you offered."

"As my queen commands, so it shall be."

ALRIK

BLOOD STILL TRICKLED from my throat. So I put it to good use while I waited for Daire to strip. I wiped fresh blood on the outside of the door in a large X and then shut and locked it. I turned, intending to pace the perimeter of the dark cell of a room, but every thought was wiped from my mind.

Naked on his knees before our queen, Daire had busy helping her remove her clothing. With his teeth. His bare, rounded buttocks a blatant invitation.

I'd fucked him many times over the years that we'd known each other. Out of every Aima I'd ever fed on, I'd fed on him the most, and I'm sure it was the same for him. Losing him would be like losing both of my limbs.

But I didn't realize that I'd still want to fuck him even after we gained a queen. I'd assumed we'd take turns pleasing our queen and that would be the end. I didn't realize I'd still want him. On his knees. For me and for her.

I had a moment to wonder if he felt the same way, or if he'd rather serve and please our queen than fuck me too, but then he glanced over his shoulder, that dimple in his cheek and twinkle in his eye telling me exactly what his intentions were.

He'd chosen to go to his knees with his back to me. For a reason.

But I didn't want to offend or neglect Shara in any way. Human sexuality was fraught with misunderstandings and inconsistencies. They didn't fuck while they fed. But for us, it went hand in hand, and there were only so many queens. Would she care that I'd be as eager to fuck Daire as herself? Would that make her feel less?

I dragged my gaze from Daire's tempting backside to check her reaction. Her eyes smoldered, her lush lips parted, and she stared at me, even as Daire pushed her shirt up and nuzzled her stomach. Shrugging off the leather jacket, she stood in order to allow him to work her jeans down her thighs.

I pulled my shirt over my head and tossed it aside. Dropped my hands to my fly. Jerked my jeans open. I could feel her holding her breath, waiting, watching, as I pulled my dick out. I gave myself a long, slow pump, watching her pupils dilate.

"Get on the bed, D."

With typical Daire flair, he did as he was told—but grabbed Shara first and tossed her up on the mattress. She squeaked with surprise, laughing as he fought to get her jeans and shoes off. Her laughter choked off into a groan when he buried his face between her thighs.

Hurrying now myself, I unlaced my boots and kicked off my pants. Her desire rose, simmering through the bond. I knelt on the bed behind Daire and ran my palm down his back.

She looked up, watching as I stroked him. I lifted my wrist to my mouth and tore the skin, letting my blood drip down on his buttocks.

He groaned, arching his back. I spread my blood across his skin, enjoying the splash of red on him. Marking him. But also arousing him to a fevered pitch. He reared back against me, leaving the feast between her thighs to lock his mouth on my wrist. I used that arm to lock him against me, his mouth around the wound, as I slowly slid into him. Since she was watching, I took my time. I pushed in a little, making him groan, denying us both. Sweet fucking torture. He rubbed his hips against me, silently begging, and his teeth dug into my skin.

She sat up in front of us and ran her hands up his thighs. "Why is he like that? So aroused?"

"Our blood can act as lubrication—and aphrodisiac. If you smeared yours on him he'd probably come on the spot."

He bit me harder, either a slight punishment for doubting his control—or an encouragement. He wanted much more than I was giving him.

I fisted my hand in his hair and gave his head a hard jerk back, locking his head against my shoulder. Her eyes flickered with surprise, maybe a touch of alarm at the show of force. "Feed, my queen. See how long he can take us both touching him before he comes."

She lightly trailed her fingers down his chest, making him shudder against me. She grazed the tip of his straining cock and a growl trickled through his lips. She hesitated, looking up at me, not him. I twisted my hand in his hair harder and thrust deeper, harder, sinking balls deep into him. "Don't worry, my queen. I've got him. Torment him all you want."

Wrapping her hand around his dick, she squeezed him, slowly drawing his length through her fingers. Daire struggled in my arms, his breathing ragged, even muffled against my arm. The more she touched him, the harder he fought me. He was stronger, now. I felt his warcat hissing and growling with anger, pacing inside the confines of his body. The warcat wanted to mate his queen. Now. Mark her with teeth and claws and blood.

But I was stronger too. My muscles swelled with power. Molten rock slid beneath my skin, hot hard stone waiting to explode. He reached back, tearing at my shoulder, and claws shredded my skin, not fingernails.

She gasped, hesitating. "I'm sorry. I didn't think he'd hurt you."

I laughed roughly and grabbed his arm, twisting it hard behind him. "I'm not hurt, my queen. This is foreplay. Daire likes me rough and mean. He likes to hurt. Don't you?"

Shara slowly backed away, sitting back against the pillows. Daire sagged against me, his fight and desire bleeding away in a surge of worry and fear through our bond. Last night, we'd been so focused on bringing her pleasure, and coming into our mutual powers, that she hadn't really seen us at our worst. Our most... real. Unpolished, raw, desire in all its violent and gory detail.

Daire liked me to hurt him, and yeah. I liked to hurt him. We liked to fight and struggle while we fucked. And I always. ALWAYS. Won. That's the way it was.

But if our half-human queen objected...

I held him closer, more shaken than I cared to admit.

I didn't want to lose what I had with Daire. Even if I gained our queen.

"Go ahead," she whispered huskily. She ran her tongue across her bottom lip and Daire whimpered. "Show me some more."

14

SHARA

I felt their indecision, a sudden trembling of uncertainty and yes, fear in our bond. They were afraid they'd offended me. It would have made me laugh if I wasn't so turned on.

Alrik stared at me, stricken at the thought of losing Daire, and it made me want to cry. "I'd never make you give him up. Why would I?"

He blew out a deep, shaking breath. Daire twisted his head around, rubbing his face on his throat. Silently asking for comfort. For his love.

"Other queens might not be so... understanding."

I shot a glare at him and fluffed up my pillows, making sure I had a good view. "Fuck other queens. I'm your queen now. And I want to see you fuck him. Fuck him exactly as you want, as you always do. I want to see what you both like. What you need. So I can give you the same."

Relief flooded our bond, followed by a tidal wave of lust. Daire lunged at me and almost escaped Alrik's grip, but he hauled the other man back by his hair.

"I will," Alrik growled in a graveled voice more rock troll

than man. "If you touch yourself while I fuck him. It'll drive him wild."

I guess it was only fair. I wanted to watch them have sex. They wanted to watch me.

I drew my legs up, spreading my thighs. Daire made a low sound like a whimper and twisted in Alrik's grip. He licked his lips, remembering what I tasted like. I'd been ridiculously close to coming earlier. A few strokes of his tongue had me quivering on the edge of an orgasm. It was embarrassing, actually, how wet and eager I was. My fingers trembled as I touched myself, praying I wouldn't come immediately.

Alrik shoved Daire's shoulders lower. His right hand gripped Daire's hip so hard his skin dented, his other forearm braced across his shoulders. He plunged deep, impaling him so hard Daire's breath whistled out and he braced his elbows on the bed, pushing back against him. Alrik thrust again, harder, making the bed thump against the wall. I couldn't believe he took him so hard, almost violently, but it was so hot. Listening to the way their flesh smacked together, their deep pants and groans. It was so... Raw.

Delicious.

Climax roared through me, making me cry out.

"Fuck, Rik, at least let me taste her."

"You'll do more than taste her. You'll make her come again."

Panting for breath, I scooted back down closer to them, but I didn't want Daire's mouth on me. I wriggled between his braced elbows and reached for his cock.

"Oh fuck," he panted. "I don't think I can stand that."

His hair tumbled down over his forehead but couldn't conceal the dark, hungry look in his eyes. Sweat glistened on his cheeks and ran in rivulets down his chest. I wrapped my legs around his hips and worked myself onto his dick. Alrik helped, moving him lower, closer, so I could take his whole length, and stopped that ferocious pounding.

Daire's chest heaved against me, every muscle trembling.

Alrik bent low over his back, pinning him against me. "Don't come until our queen has her fill."

I thought he meant until I came again, and maybe he did, but he also meant blood. Because he dragged his fangs across Daire's throat so I could feed from him too.

Blood dripped onto my breasts, each drop like liquid sunlight sizzling my skin. I hooked my arm around Daire's neck and levered myself up so I could get my mouth on the wound. Alrik thrust deep, shoving Daire deeper into me, making us both moan. It suddenly dawned on me that he was fucking us both, even though he wasn't inside me. He used Daire's body to give me pleasure too. He ground hard against Daire's buttocks, which pressed his pelvis against my clit. I arched against them, circling my hips, driving our need higher. Blood burned on my skin. Alrik's. Daire's. Their blood flowed together, mixing into a combustible intoxicating blend on my skin that made me rub my breasts against Daire, smearing him too.

"It burns," I gasped. Even as I wanted more of their blood. It felt like hot wax dripping onto my skin. I could only imagine what it'd be like to have them coat me head to toe in their blood.

"Yes," Alrik growled out. Through our bond, I saw an image of me, coated in blood like something from a horror movie. It pushed me over the edge. I threw my head back, my throat hurting with the cry of release that ripped from my lungs. Daire took that invitation and sank his fangs into my throat. Another wave of pleasure pounded through me. Through him. Through Alrik. Like dominoes.

Gasping, we lay together, the three of us still entwined while we recovered. Sweat and blood and semen scented the air. I breathed deeper, taking them into my lungs.

Daire licked his punctures in my throat and made a pleased hum against my skin. "That was... incredible."

"Except Alrik didn't feed." He'd fallen off a bit to the right, his face planted in the pillow beside me. At my words, he stirred, but didn't lift his head. "Rik? Do you need my blood?"

He turned his head enough to smile at me, his eyes dazed and dark with pleasure, still high on sex and endorphins. "That's the first time you've called me Rik. I like it," he said before I could ask. "Later, my queen. I'm fine at the moment. How do you feel? Did you get enough blood from us?"

"I don't know." That made both men scramble up like I'd goosed them with a cattle prod, their brows furrowed. Laughing, I sat up and pointed down at the pillows. "Both of you lie down. I want to look you over."

Two big muscular bodies stretched out on the mattress for my perusal. I climbed over Daire so I was between them. I picked up Alrik's injured arm and licked the still bleeding slash Daire's teeth had torn into him. "Will this heal?"

"It'll be gone by morning," he rumbled, his eyes heavy even though we'd just fucked each other senseless. "Let me—"

"No," I broke in. "This is enough."

I probed the jagged edges of the wound with my tongue and he groaned, but not with pain. I closed my eyes, gripping him in my teeth, pretending that I'd been able to bite him like this. That I had made this wound.

I tried not to share how afraid I was that I'd never be able to bite them, but the bond held no secrets. He drew me down against his chest and kissed my forehead. "You will," he whispered. "I have no doubt."

"Just your luck that you found the last Isador heir, who's half human and doesn't even have fangs."

Daire cuddled into Alrik's side, looping his arm over my back. "Our virgin vampire queen needs no fangs to keep us happy."

I snorted, rubbing my nose against Alrik's chest hair. "I'm not a virgin any longer."

"But you're our vampire queen. And you will be able to mark us. I have no doubt."

15

ALRIK

Before waking our queen, I watched her sleep for several moments. Her hair was a tangled mess. Her skin smeared with drying, flaking blood. She had one arm up over her eyes, even though it wasn't bright in this room. How could it be with no windows? It was as if her body knew it was full day outside and was still shielding itself. She had one leg out from beneath the sheets, but kept the rest of her body covered. Not from chill, since I'd noticed she was rarely cold. She'd only wanted the leather jacket because we'd had one and she loved the smell and look.

I set the cup of coffee on the nightstand and carefully sat on the edge of the bed. At least we hadn't destroyed this one. Through the bond, I felt for her mind, trying to see how close to waking she might be. If she was truly exhausted and wanted her rest, I'd leave her to sleep the rest of the day. We had no pressing needs. Just a desire to treat our queen like the extremely wealthy and previously neglected young woman who'd not yet enjoyed the privilege that her wealth and birthright provided.

She felt far away, as if she'd traveled a great distance in her sleep. I laid my hand on her arm, using the physical to connect to the metaphysical.

I was suddenly in her dream. A silent watcher in the shadowed night.

SHE STOOD at the iron gate, fully illuminated by the large security light, her arm stretched through the bars, reaching for something outside. Calling.

Darkness stirred. Something evil. I could feel its hunger and dark rage. She could too, but she wasn't afraid. She didn't yank her arm back or step away from the flimsy gate. I smelled her blood, saw it dripping down her wrist to dot the snow with crimson. Each drop hit the ground and roses burst up in full glorious bloom, their perfume covering the stench of the monster on the other side of the fence.

"It's all right," she crooned to the thing like it was a baby and she wanted to cuddle it. "I'm here to free you."

Chains rattled and teeth gnashed like clanging swords. A massive shadow stretched toward her, drawn by her blood and sweet spirit.

I lunged forward, but I didn't think I was going to make it. I could see the red glare of its eyes. Those vicious teeth nearing her flesh.

GASPING, I jerked out of the dream and pulled her with me. I had her on my lap, pressed against my heaving chest. Daire came running, though I didn't know if I'd shouted for help or if he'd felt something through our bond. He charged into the room, ketars on each hand ready to slice whatever threatened us into tiny pieces.

"What?" She cried out, looking around wildly. "What's wrong? Are they here?"

I clutched her hard, trying to settle myself so I didn't alarm her further. "You were dreaming."

"Dreaming? Then why are you so alarmed?"

I forced myself to loosen my grip on her, but I held Daire's gaze so he would know the extent to which we needed to guard our queen. Even in her sleep. "Do you remember the dream?"

She was silent a moment. "I was outside. Calling to something on the other side of the fence."

"Yes. Something that was… evil."

Her head tipped to the side, and I felt her sifting through her memory of the dream. "It wasn't Greyson, the monster that killed my parents. Was it?"

"I don't think so. At least I didn't recognize him or sense him. This was something else entirely."

She shrugged and sat up, reaching for the cup of coffee. I resisted the urge to clutch her tighter, refusing to let her go. "It was just a dream."

"Nothing is just a dream for you, my queen." Daire removed the ketars and hung them on his hips. "The goddess gave you many powers. Walking the nightscape in dream form is one of them."

I didn't have to warn him that we had to start guarding her dreams as well as her waking moments. If she managed to call something evil like that to her side, even in her dreams, we had to be ready to defend her.

She sipped the coffee with a pleased hum that made me go rock hard in my jeans despite my fear for her safety. "I wasn't scared. Not like the monsters."

"That doesn't mean this thing you called wasn't as dangerous." Maybe it was my lingering fear, but I pressed my lips against her shoulder and inhaled her scent. She smelled so good, warm and sweet and somehow luxuriously sexy. I wanted to rub on her like Daire's warcat and make sure she carried my scent. "You will be calling Blood to your side. Let's not call up a bunch of nightmare creatures that are just as dangerous as the thralls."

"Mmmm hmmm," she giggled. "Nightmare creatures like a rock troll and a warcat. Mustn't call up anything else."

Daire went down to his knees in front of us and rubbed his

face against the tops of her thighs. "We thought to take you shopping but I'm starting to think that was a bad idea."

I agreed. Wholeheartedly. But our queen stood, gently pulling away.

"I need to use the bathroom."

I followed on her heels, still hungry for her scent. Her skin. Her warmth. I wanted to bury myself in her all over again. I laid my forehead against the door, waiting for her to come back out.

"Are you all right?" Daire whispered. "Rik? Rik!"

"What?" Something poked me in the back. Hard. I jerked my head up and glared at him, my lips twisting in a snarl.

"Something's wrong with you."

I shook my head, trying to shake the rage crawling through me. It felt like millions of fire ants marched through my veins. "Does she smell different to you?"

"Not different. Just… tasty. Like I'm not going to be able to get my fill."

"Yeah." I blew out a sigh and dragged a hand through my hair. "Maybe it was that dream. Fuck, Daire, you should have felt that thing she was calling out of the night. I've never felt anything like it."

The door opened and she jumped a little, her eyes widening to see us standing there. Then her eyes narrowed on me, which made me guiltily back up a step. "That's creepy."

"Forgive me, my queen. I'm feeling… unsettled."

"I used that trick you showed me to clean my clothes, but I still think I want a nice long bath tonight."

"As you wish, of course."

She hesitated, watching me, and I wanted to drop to my knees and plant my face against her stomach. "A little space would be good."

I suddenly realized I was completely blocking the door. No wonder she stood there looking at me strangely. I ducked my head and stepped aside, letting Daire take over the small talk.

He'd made breakfast, but all she wanted was coffee. She sat on the leather couch in the sitting room and pulled her knees up to her chest. Her cheeks looked a little pale to me. I wanted to touch her forehead, search our bond for any ailment, but I'd already alarmed her with my possessiveness.

Daire rattled off a list of shops we intended to take her to, asking her frivolous questions to make her laugh. The more he flirted and giggled with her, the more silent and grim I became. She needed that lightness. I got it. He'd be able to tease and coerce her where I would only make her dig her heels in, even if in the end, the result was the same.

It wasn't like me to feel so... jealous. Petty. Shame tightened my throat, which only made me feel worse. I was her alpha Blood. I had to act like it. I had to use her other Blood to their best advantage. Even if that meant I was excluded. It'd never bothered me before.

Daire's flirtatious mischief hadn't offended me in the slightest last night.

But right now...

I wanted to fucking rip his head off.

1 6

SHARA

I didn't really want to go shopping, especially this close to Christmas. The streets and shops would be packed and I'd never been comfortable around lots of people. I didn't think that feeling would suddenly dissipate just because I'd discovered I was Isis's last heir. But Daire was so excited to take me somewhere new, and yeah, part of me had to admit I was curious how it'd feel when I could walk into any store I wanted and buy anything that caught my fancy without batting an eyelash.

Alrik, on the other hand, had turned into a granite lump without shifting into his stone troll. I wasn't sure what was the matter with him. He'd been appalled by my dream. Maybe I'd unconsciously broken some terrible rule by calling the creature. I hadn't meant to. I just felt it out there. Alone, wild, tormented, enraged. I could feel it screaming in silent agony that no one could hear but me. How could I not reach out to it and try to help?

Not it. Him. He'd definitely been male.

Alrik had said I should call more Blood to me. How was that different than what I'd done last night? If I'd felt him or Daire prowling around in the night as their beasts, would I have been too afraid to reach for them too? I knew better than that. Something inside them resonated in me too, even when they weren't human and didn't look human. The same as the man from this latest dream.

I stood beside him on the front steps, waiting while Daire brought Mom's red Jaguar around. Alrik kept looking at me, his eyes flickering as if he wanted to say something, but didn't want to upset me. Or offend me. And then he'd turn aside, his jaws working as he bit back whatever he'd wanted to say.

I slipped my hand into his and his head whipped around, his eyes locking on my face. "Are we all right?"

His eyes narrowed and he took a menacing step closer. Yes, menacing, bumping into me in an aggressive way that sent a hot wave of sudden desire flooding through me. I couldn't help but remember the way he'd fucked Daire last night. So hard, brutal, raw. He'd never touched me like that.

And I wanted it. I wanted him.

"Why wouldn't we be?" He retorted, though his words were quiet. "Are *you* upset with *me*?"

I leaned into him, pressing my breasts against his arm. My nipples ached, so surely he could feel how hard they were. "Does this feel like I'm upset with you?"

He threaded his fingers in my hair, the same as he'd done to Daire last night. But he didn't jerk my head back, baring my throat.

Daire jumped out of the car and swept the rear passenger door open. "Ready, my queen?"

Alrik released my hair but he didn't step back. He watched me slide into the car with heavy-lidded eyes and he growled at Daire, though I wasn't sure why.

They'd fucked each other last night, but today, they were aggressive to each other. It didn't make sense.

I felt uneasy and tense all the way to downtown Kansas City, even though Alrik sat beside me and held my hand as if nothing was wrong. I just felt out of sorts. Vaguely achy and disinterested and even weepy for no particular reason. And then it hit me.

PMS. My period was due to start. I broke out in a cold sweat and my stomach rolled queasily.

"Shara? Are you all right?"

I forced a small smile. "I'm fine. I just remembered that I get car sick easily."

Daire met my gaze through the rear-view mirror, dimple flashing in his cheek. "Then you should ride up here on the way home. That might help with the motion sickness."

I nodded, and heard a small noise from Alrik, almost like a muttered curse. I glanced at him, but he was looking out the window.

I concentrated on our bond, trying to listen without being intrusive. His emotions surged like an angry sea. Jealousy rose like a tidal wave, only to crush into a downward spiral of guilt. Then anger at himself. And confusion. He was just as confused about what he was feeling as I was. That helped, some.

Maybe he was feeling some odd effect from my PMS? It was like my emotions were magnified in him, only more toward anger.

And lust, I decided, feeling the surge as I climbed out of the car. I glanced back over my shoulder and his eyes were locked to my ass.

The Power and Light District was festively lit, even during the daytime. I took a deep breath, hoping to calm my social anxiety before it got out of hand. I didn't want to affect Alrik even more, or he might stride into the crowd slinging bodies out of my way. Even Daire was feisty after I insisted he leave his ketars in the car, but he offered me his arm, so I linked elbows with him and reached for Alrik too, tugging him close. He growled at Daire over my head, but he just winked back at him.

We ate some fantastic barbecue and window shopped for a couple of hours. I bought a couple of books—hardcovers, something I never would have splurged on before, both because of the expense and the weight in case I needed to bolt. My shiny gold card worked effortlessly. We found a trendy boutique shop selling women's clothes, and Daire insisted I try on practically everything in the store. At least that's what it felt like. Once he got me in a dressing room, he refused to let me out by bringing arm loads for me to try on. Alrik sat glowering on a cushioned bench in the center. A sales assistant started to come over to ask if I needed any help, took one look at the mountain of a man outside my stall door, and quickly buzzed past to help someone else.

The stack of things Daire wanted me to buy was almost as tall as me. "I don't need this much stuff," I protested, trying to figure out where I'd even put that much. I didn't have a closet in the tower, though my old room downstairs had a large walk-in that was mostly empty.

"Yes, you do." He waved the assistant over. "She'll take these things. Could they be delivered for her later today?"

The woman's eyes rounded at the huge pile, and I could almost see the cash register cha-chinging in her head. "Of course, I'm sure we can arrange that. If my manager can't, I'll bring them to you myself."

She started to gather up all the hangers, but Alrik slammed his hand down on the stack. He went down through several layers until he found a particular item, pulling it out even though it messed up the top clothes. "Put this one on."

Something in me bristled at his tone. The queen in me raising her head, tipping her chin, refusing to bow. The woman took the dress and raced up to the cash register so she could ring it up, and then brought the dress back. "You might be cold in it. It's not really a winter dress."

I stared at him, while the lady stood there with the dress, awkwardly looking back and forth between us. I didn't look at the dress—I wasn't even sure which one it was. That wasn't the point. If he thought he could start dictating to me what I could wear... That was going to stop. Now.

I'd never had a boyfriend, let alone a date a full-grown man. But even if I was just an ordinary human woman dating the average Joe, there was no way in hell I'd let him order me about. "Just because you've had your dick in me doesn't mean you can tell me what to do. Let alone what to wear."

Alrik bowed his head and shocked the hell out of me by going to one knee before me despite the crowded store and the goggling sales person. "Forgive me, my queen. I don't know what came over me."

I stepped closer to him and wrapped my arm around his straining shoulders. He buried his face against my stomach, and despite his apology, I felt his teeth on my belly. He even started to nuzzle lower, as if he'd bury his face in my pussy right here in the store. Before things got out of hand, I drew back, took the diaphanous dress from the woman, and stepped into the dressing room.

"She'll need matching shoes," Daire said to the woman.

"Oh! Yes, I know just the pair."

I stepped out of my jeans and checked my underwear to be safe. Crap, I'd started already. I hadn't brought my backpack along. Usually I would have put in a tampon right away, even if I wasn't flowing much. It seemed to help keep my scent under control so I could get away from the monsters during the day and hide somewhere new before nightfall. It didn't always work, but it did seem to help.

I needed to stock up on the way home. Blowing out a sigh, I tried to think of a creative way to ask two healthy males to stop for tampons at the drug store as I balled up the stained undies and dropped them in the little waste basket. Leaving behind a decoy to attract the monsters to my old location usually helped me slip away undetected. Though going commando in a slinky dress was not the smartest thing I'd ever done.

Plus I missed my pockets. I couldn't carry my knife or a weapon of any kind in a stupid dress. The material was so thin and sheer that it felt like I was wrapped in spider webs and moon-light. Long sleeves fluttered about my wrists, while the bodice hugged my breasts and nipped in my waist. The skirt was longer in the back than the front, almost to the floor, and several sheer layers that swished about my ankles and thighs when I walked.

It should have looked messy or slutty, but somehow managed to look dreamy instead. I looked like a silver fairy princess. I pulled my hair out of the pony tail and fluffed it up a bit with my fingers, but it still looked heavy and flat. Closing my eyes, I tried to envision loose curls about my shoulders, drawing on the magic that lived inside me. Nothing happened at first, and it took me a second to realize why.

Blood. I needed blood to make my power come to life.

I wasn't going to bleed, or make someone else bleed, just to fix my hair.

But then I remembered my period had started. Would that be enough? I reached through my body, feeling for that tiny bit of blood energy. However, when I tapped it, I almost short-circuited myself. Holy shit. My hair sprang up around my head, my nerves zinged, muscles twitched. Daire and Alrik bolted toward me, banging into each other in their urgency to reach me in the tiny dressing room.

"I'm fine," I said, though my voice rang in my head, making me wince.

"What the fuck was that?" Alrik reached toward me, but Daire snagged his arm. There was a bit of a wrestling match, biceps bulging, and Alrik ended up shoving him aside, but in the end, Daire won, because Alrik didn't touch me.

It was a good thing. I still felt like I throbbed with electricity. My skin felt tender, as if I'd heated myself up too much or stuck my finger in a light socket. Note to self: period blood was some powerful shit. "I was trying to fix my hair and um… That didn't work."

Daire snorted. "Yeah, no shit. Your hair looks like you've

been riding on the back of one of our bikes for days with no helmet, while we went as fast as possible."

Closing my eyes, I concentrated very very carefully and smoothed my hands over my hair, bringing the static electricity down to at least smooth, though wild, curls. "Better?"

"Yes," Alrik said gruffly.

"Try these," the sales woman waved some strappy silver heels between my two guys. "I've also got some rhinestone ones, but they're a bit loud. I think they'd detract from the simplicity of the gown."

"Thank you." I took the shoes, but the look on Alrik's face said he wasn't done with the interrogation. He sensed something was off with me, but what could I say? I didn't want to blurt out that I was bleeding between my legs and I needed a tampon. That was just... crude. Besides, for all I knew, periods were a human thing that he wouldn't have a clue about. How embarrassing would that be trying to explain to a vampire?

I put the shoes on and took a few experimental, wobbly steps. They looked fantastic in the mirror, but I didn't want to break my neck just to look fabulous. Though my legs went on for miles. Turning, I faced my men. "What do you think?"

"You look like the queen you are." Alrik's voice carried throughout the common area of the dressing room. A few women's heads popped over stall doors, and the sales person's eyes were bugging out at the thought I might be someone famous.

"Your Majesty." Daire took my hand and bowed low, kissing my knuckles. "You look like you're ready to go to the ball. I think there's a bar with dancing at the end of the street. Do you want to check it out?"

Dancing. At a bar. With two gorgeous men. In a dreamy dress. Of course I wanted to go. Duh. As long as I got home soon before I had a real mess to deal with. I looked at the sales person. "Can you go ahead and ring the rest up, or do I need to stop back by to pay for everything else?"

"I'll ring everything up, and I'll bring a receipt for you to sign when I drop everything off. Does that work?"

She stumbled over the last few words, as if trying to decide whether to call me ma'am, miss, or worse, Your Majesty like Daire. "Perfect. Thank you for your help. Daire, could you make sure she has our address?"

Alrik helped me put my leather jacket back on while Daire jotted down where we lived. The sales lady frowned at the black leather. "I have a very classy wool dress coat…"

"No thanks," I said, headed to the door. "I like the leather."

Outside, the air had a bite of snow. It wasn't quite four o'clock yet, but dark fell by five this time of the year. Daire ran to throw my stuff in the car, unable to do that quick zip-vanish thing with all these witnesses. "I want to be home well before dark."

Alrik tipped my chin up with his thumb, his fingers gentle even though his eyes glittered with emotion. Anger, that I was still afraid, and still that odd aggression, like a bull moose staking his territory. "You have no reason to be afraid of the dark any longer. We will protect you. Even at full dark. Even if you're filling the night with the scent of blood. Nothing will touch you. End of story."

"I don't doubt you in the slightest. But why risk injury or death just to walk around at a club for the night?"

"You think too little of us if you fear a few thralls would hurt a Blood seriously enough to put us or you at risk."

He hadn't seen the frantic, frenzied way the monsters got when they finally caught up to me. The ones they'd seen in Arkansas had been driven to get me, yes—but they'd still acted with cunning. When my period was going full force, their efforts to get to me always took on a way more sinister, out-of-control madness. Remembering made me shiver. I just wanted to be home, locked up in four walls, with my two guys wrapped around me. Only then would I feel safe.

He drew me closer, wrapping his arms around me. "Are you cold?"

"No. Just scared."

He glowered down at me as if I'd mortally offended him.

Not even breathing quickly after the trip back to us, Daire slapped him on the back and took my hand. "Stop glaring and let's go have some fun."

ALRIK

I DON'T KNOW why my anger still simmered just beneath the surface. When I opened the door to the bar Daire pointed out, I had to deliberately think about opening the door gently, not tearing it off its hinges. Music throbbed in the air, some band I didn't recognize. A few people sat at the industrial-looking bar and a couple of tables, but the place wasn't packed yet. Come five o'clock I imagined this place would be humming. So probably a good idea to head out well before dark, though I didn't appreciate the fact that she was scared to be out at night.

My queen was not scared. Ever.

Daire snagged her hands and pulled her out onto the empty dance floor. "Get us some drinks!"

Deep breath. Relax the fists. Try not to growl at the man behind the bar who was looking at my queen appreciatively. I ordered three drafts, since I had no idea what Shara would like, and carried the mugs to a table in the corner near the rear exit sign. Then I sat and watched her. Everyone in the bar did.

She was fucking beautiful for one thing, especially in that silver dress. Daire whirled her around, making her laugh, and I swear my heart grew ten sizes too big for my chest. She looked at me, her brow furrowed, as though worried what I thought. Afraid I was jealous. And I was, but not for the reasons she feared. She should laugh and dance, every day, every minute. She shouldn't be afraid or solemn.

And Daire would always be the one to make her laugh. Not me.

The song ended so they headed toward our table. A few people clapped as she walked by, startling her into a blush that only made her more gorgeous. My fangs and dick both ached. I hadn't fed last night. Hadn't needed to. But I was definitely feeling the lack tonight. Maybe that explained my bad mood.

She took a sip of the foamy beer and made a face. Daire started to slide out of the booth to get her another drink, but she stopped him with a hand on his arm. "This is fine. I've just never had beer for before."

"I can get you a glass of wine. Red or white?"

"I don't know. I haven't had that either until last night. I haven't been in a place where I felt safe enough to risk impairing my senses with alcohol."

"Uh oh, now you've done it." Daire winked at me. "Now you've given us an excuse to get you totally wasted."

"Not out here," she whispered, looking around. "What time is it?"

I clenched my jaws so hard my teeth ached.

"We've only been here fifteen minutes," Daire replied. "At least drink some more of your beer."

She looked at me, her eyes gleaming. "And dance with Rik before we leave."

I had four left feet and moved as gracefully as a mountain when I didn't have a weapon in my hand or an enemy to eliminate. "As my queen wishes."

More people started to stream in, keeping my senses on high alert, even though I didn't expect a thrall to just walk into a human bar. I could feel her anxiety leaking through our bond, too. Her flight response was screaming that it was time to move. Time to leave. Hide. Now. When Daire drained his mug in several long gulps, I knew it was affecting him too.

"I need to hit the rest room," she said.

Daire scooted to the edge of the bench and helped her up. I stood too, not willing to let her out of my sight, not with her fear so high. "Watch our drinks," I told him, and then followed her to the opposite side of the building. She hesitated at the entrance to a dark hallway. No windows and very little light made it hard to see for human eyes, but she shouldn't have any issues. Concerned, I stepped closer to her, letting her feel the heat and nearness of my body. "What is it?"

I could hear her heart thumping quicker. "I don't know. It just doesn't feel right down there. Can we go? Please?"

I intended to step around her and investigate that hallway, because nothing was going to make her beg. Nothing. But she turned to face me, pressing against my body, her arms coming around me.

"I don't want to have to leave Kansas City until we *want* to leave."

"Why would we have to leave?"

She pressed her lips to my throat. "Because you get into some bloody fight with a monster, with all these witnesses to take pictures and post online. Or because you called me 'Your Majesty' in front of that sales lady. People talk, and they're curious, and with today's technology, there is no such thing as a secret. Not for long."

I tightened my arms around her, lifting her slightly so my dick nestled into the sweet softness of her body. Her breath caught. Her fingers tightened. I felt her teeth—very human teeth, sadly—at my throat and something cracked inside me. I had her up against the wall, her thighs open, my hand sliding up under that gorgeous dress.

Skin. Pubes. Not underwear.

Fucking hell. My queen was walking around completely bare. Evidently my brain shut off because all the blood in my body had drained south. Worse, my power surged and rock hardened beneath my skin—and not just in my pants. "Where are your panties?" I rasped out, trying to get myself back under control before I transformed into the rock troll and became a national news sensation.

"My period started and I tossed them in the trash at the clothes store."

I had to have missed some words. Misunderstood. Period. I knew what that was, but... but...

I had to know. I slid a finger deeper and found wetness. Not her desire, though. My skin knew her blood. Cells in my fingers were already eagerly trying to absorb her essence, her blood, her power through osmosis.

Fuck.

I swept her up against me and sent Daire an urgent warning. *:Get the fucking car.:*

I didn't stop to look for him, but raced for the exit, ignoring the fire alarm that sounded. Tires screeched as the Jaguar came tearing down the alley, slowing only enough for me to jump in. In moments, we were a red blur racing down the freeway.

Shaking, I held her on my lap, fighting back my urges. These urges went way beyond desire and sex to animalistic mating. No wonder I'd been on edge all fucking day. No wonder I wanted to tear even Daire limb from limb. And no wonder she'd been so anxious about staying out after dark.

"Sorry," she whispered, in a small voice that fucking wrecked me.

I tipped her face up and pressed my forehead to hers. "Don't you ever apologize for something you have no control over."

"But this is bad, right? The monsters are worse than ever when I have my period."

My throat felt like I'd swallowed razor blades. "It's a fucking miracle you lived through a single period, Shara. I mean it. This is not a regular occurrence for Aima females. I had no idea you were menstruating or I never would have suggested a trip outside your house. We need a nest more than ever."

"How often do you bleed?" Daire asked from the driver's seat.

She blew out a sigh. "Every fucking month. That's why I moved so often. I'd run during the day and find a new place to hole up for the night, but when I'm bleeding, no place is safe for more than a few hours."

"Every month?" Daire sounded like I'd wrapped a fist around his throat and was slowly choking him to death. "Fuck. Rik, how…? I can't…?"

"Yeah." I carefully set her off me onto the seat so we weren't touching. Or I was going to be buried to the hilt right here in her mother's car. "Quick Aima biology lesson. We're vampires, right? So you can imagine what blood is doing to us."

"Even… *that* blood?"

I had to breathe deeply, counting to ten. My head kept turning toward her, my body trying to turn in the seat, reach for her, touch her. It was absolutely involuntary. I flattened my palms on my thighs and focused on my hands…

Mistake. Huge. Because I could see her blood on my right hand. The only thing that kept me from licking it off and coming like a hurricane all over her was the unease and hint of disgust in her voice. "Yes. Even more so. Because that means you're fertile."

"Aima women don't have regular periods." Daire seemed to be faring a little better than me—but he had to have the gas pedal pressed to the floor as fast as we were flying. "When they're ready to conceive a child, they go into heat and bleed. That's their bodies' way of attracting Aima males. As a queen, your blood is already a heady aphrodisiac that carries all the nuclear punch of Isis's legacy. Now add in menstrual heat, and we're going to fucking lose our minds, Shara. Seriously, I don't know how we're going to survive."

Sweat trickled down my forehead and my hands throbbed from gripping my own thighs. "Let alone monthly."

Daire let out a sound suspiciously like a whimper.

"I'm half human though," Shara said, her voice quivering. "Human women are glad when they get their period—that means they're *not* pregnant." Her breath caught and her voice elevated an octave. "Does that mean I could get pregnant? Now? Or does it mean I'm human enough that I'm *not* pregnant? I love you guys, but I so do not want a baby right now."

My breathing was quickly becoming a desperate wheeze. "That. Would be. Disastrous."

"No nest," Daire ground out. "Fuck. We are so screwed. We need help, Rik. Bad."

For the first time since finding our queen, I suddenly wished we weren't alone. Because he was absolutely correct.

We were fucked.

17

SHARA

The more freaked out my men became, the more I wanted to laugh. Even though I was scared shitless. If these two magnificent, powerful men were scared, I was fucking terrified.

I reached down and felt around in my jeans Daire had tossed in earlier to find the phone Gina had given me.

"Your Majesty," Gina answered immediately. "How may I be of assistance?"

"I need to see a doctor. That we can trust, who knows about our kind."

"Are you injured?" Her volume increased. "Where are you?"

"I'm fine, at the moment, but we have some… concerns. I need to talk to someone who knows both human and Aima reproductive biologies. I'd like some tests ran."

"Ah. I see. Yes, I've got someone we can trust. I'll call her and meet you at the house as soon as possible."

Impressed, I let out a soft whistle. "You can get a doctor that fast?"

"Your Majesty." Gina sounded put out. "Your doubt wounds me."

We'd barely pulled into the garage when Gina's familiar sedan parked at the curb. I started to get out of the car to greet them, but Alrik hauled me up and ran for the house. Daire sprinted ahead and got the door open for us. He didn't stop, but took me directly up the two flights of stairs to the tower room.

He tossed me on the bed like I was a flaming hot potato and retreated to pant against the wall. Sweat trickled down his face, his T-shirt was glued to him, and his jeans strained at the crotch.

"Fuck, don't you dare look at my dick." His head fell back and he grimaced like I'd started pulling his fingernails off with a pair of pliers.

Of course then I couldn't stop looking at him.

I heard Daire and the two women tromping up the stairs so I finally dragged my gaze away from the impressive log in Alrik's pants. Daire hit the door and didn't pause once his eyes locked on me. Alrik snagged him by the back of the neck and dragged him back against the wall with him. They scuffled a moment, Daire fighting to escape, but then Alrik roared through the bond, a deep, bone-rattling growl that stilled Daire's beast.

"Your Majesty, this is my good friend, Dr. Mala Borcht," Gina said. "I can personally vouch for her discretion and expertise in all things Aima. Would you like for me to remain or wait downstairs?"

"You can stay. You all can stay. You should all know what's going on because we will be attacked, and it will be bad."

Alrik growled a warning and nodded. "I feel them drawing near already, and if our queen's instincts were correct, something threatened her in broad daylight at a public bar downtown."

"In daylight?" Dr. Borcht tapped her perfectly manicured nails against her chin. "A threat you, the alpha Blood, could not sense? Then it wasn't a thrall."

Alrik's cheeks flushed a dull red but he nodded. "I sensed nothing but she didn't feel safe. Then I found why and we left immediately. I didn't investigate to find the cause. I felt it better to remove her from the situation and retreat to the closest thing we have as a nest."

"Very smart," Dr. Borcht replied. "So, Your Majesty, what concerns you?"

"My period started today."

Gina gasped beneath her breath, but I heard her whispered prayer. *"Blessed be, Goddess, may your line live forever."*

"I see. So you're wondering if that's a good thing, with your human parentage, or a risky thing, with your Aima mother," Dr. Borcht replied. "Yes, a very interesting case to be sure. Is menstruation a new development for you?"

"Not at all. I've had a period every month since I was fifteen."

Her eyes widened and tiny fine white lines formed around her mouth. "Every month?"

"Without fail."

"I'm sorry, Your Majesty, but I'm wondering how it's possible that you're even still alive."

"Exactly," Alrik muttered, running a hand over his head. "Fuck, the more I think about it, the more pissed off I get."

"That's not good for you right now," Dr. Borcht said. "The more emotions you feel, the harder it'll be for you to control your urges. I'd ask you to take a walk but I know you'd refuse."

"I won't let her out of my sight," Alrik retorted.

Dr. Borcht held her hands up soothingly. "No one's asking you to leave. But try to keep your emotions leveled and calm."

Turning back to me, she set a cute typewriter purse on the bed and opened it, revealing a well-stocked medical bag despite its size. "I'm assuming since this isn't a new occurrence, that your period means you're not pregnant or in heat, but the opposite, the same as any human female. But there are some blood tests I can run to be sure."

"How long will it take?"

She pulled out a syringe and several vials. "Oh, this evening.

We failed to mention that I run a state-of-the-art lab in Overland Park."

When the needle sank into my arm, a growl trickled out of Alrik's lips. Daire pressed against him, a hard hand on his shoulder. I don't know if it was the blood... or the small prick of pain they had to have felt. I might have been a vampire queen, but I still fucking hated needles.

"In the meantime, I recommend you stay enclosed here in the house until you decide where to establish your nest. Have you put out a call for more Blood?"

"No. At least I don't think I have. How do I do that?"

"It's not exactly something you *do*. In my limited understanding as only a very small fraction of my family tree claims to be Aima, it's more of a feeling. An existence on your part, and your need for protection. More Blood should be headed to you, and if you're half as strong as I suspect you'll be, easily a dozen or twenty Blood will come to your aid. If you deliberately think of your need for protection, feeling and searching for them, they should come."

"But when?" Daire paced back and forth, his steps as lithe and silent as a panther. "We need help now. We need guards. We need someone at the perimeter."

I tried not to remember the dream from this morning, because it'd upset Alrik so much. But I couldn't help but wonder what... or who... I'd been calling. Another Blood? Or something else?

I distinctly remembered the sound of chains, combined with the smell of something... scaled. Snake? Dragon? Something else entirely? I really had no idea. I didn't know if the thing I'd called was a true monster—or if that was merely the mythological creature he'd transform into once I brought him into full power.

I'd found Alrik and Daire by searching in the night, using that internal sense of tapestry, a rolling landscape in my head. Closing my eyes, I concentrated on my surroundings. Night approached. I could feel it like a shadow creeping closer to the house, almost ready to engulf us. At the fringe of the approaching darkness, I felt them. Monsters. So many. I don't think I'd ever seen so many at once.

:Are you seeing this?: I asked through the bond to both Blood.

:Yes,: Alrik replied grimly, his bond shimmering like a steel blade in my head. Hard, angry, sharp, ready for damage. *:Where's the master thrall?:*

Panic crawled through my head, making it difficult to concentrate. Externally, I heard Daire telling the women they had to leave. Now. To get the blood work done as quickly as possible, before they were trapped here with us. Internally, I felt the clumps of monsters closing in. I touched each one, cringing and shuddering at the foulness leaking off them. But none of those evil smudges were Greyson. He was always there with them, sending them after me. So where was he?

"Wait." My eyes flew open. Dr. Borcht and Gina paused at the door. "Where's my mother buried?"

"She wanted to be buried here on the property, but even the immense Isador wealth couldn't make that happen. She's buried with your father at the Stuller Cemetery. You passed it on the way in from the freeway."

"Thanks."

I closed my eyes, feeling down the road, searching for where that abandoned chapel must be. Distantly, I heard the women leaving. I felt Alrik close, hovering, angry, and yes, scared for me. Worried because I only had two Blood. And while he would die to keep me safe, if he died…

A sob escaped. I felt such agony, crippling searing grief. It took me a moment to realize it wasn't mine.

Greyson. He crawled across holy ground, struggling, bleeding and howling with pain, trying to reach my mother's grave. His skin blistered and split, black blood leaking onto the ground, and he writhed in the snow. He didn't care about the pain. He only wanted to be with her. To die on her grave. Maybe in death he could at last be with her.

But there was no release of death for him. He couldn't die, yet he couldn't live without her either. He couldn't even reach her grave before being forced to retreat. He was trapped on this earth, filled with rage and hate. She'd taken everything away from him when she'd left London. His power, his love, her blood, the gift of his own to her, the companionship with the other Blood, his brothers.

He turned, sensing my touch, and glared toward the house with those demon-red eyes. I couldn't read his thoughts, not like my Blood, but his emotions leaked like poison, fouling everything he touched. If he couldn't have my mother, then he'd have me. And if he couldn't have me, then my Blood wouldn't have me either. He'd at least do that much. He'd show them what it was like to lose their queen.

I heard a scream in the night, a panther-like shriek. Then the ground rumbled, the three-dimensional map in my head quivering like an earthquake. Even without touching Alrik's bond, I knew that was his rock troll, stomping and slamming his fists against the ground, cracking it open as a warning. They were ready to defend me. They were ready to fight.

They just needed one thing.

My blood.

18

ALRIK

My queen opened her eyes and scooted back on the bed, opening her arms and thighs to me. I could already smell her heat, mixed with the intoxicating scent of her blood.

I froze, afraid to move. Afraid I'd crack her into a thousand pieces if I touched her while my rock troll thumped around in my body, slamming boulder fists against my skin like he'd tear me open if I didn't transform soon.

She tipped her head to the side, exposing the long column of her throat. So vulnerable. So trusting. So beautiful. "Before this fight, you need to feed. You need to be as strong as possible."

Yet I held my position, probably denting the shape of my shoulders into the plaster walls with my determination to stay put. "If you're breeding..."

"I'm not. At least I don't think so. And if I am..." She shrugged, keeping her face averted, and she drew her legs back together slightly. "Unless you mind the blood. I just thought—"

I slammed into her, literally. Fangs in her throat. Dick in her pussy. Her breath rushed out on a groan. Her thighs came up

138

around my waist, hugging me close. Power exploded through me and for a moment, I thought I'd die with the sheer strength of the surge. The top of my skull felt like it'd blown off. My nerves screamed with sensation. The rock troll bulged inside me, desperate to transform, ready to fuck, fight, and then fuck again. Gritting my teeth, I fought to keep the beast contained inside me. The size of that troll—it'd tear her apart.

Fireworks exploded behind my eyelids. My skin felt scorched, like I'd fallen into the sun itself and disintegrated. And my dick felt like a claymore, long, hard steel, plunging deep, determined to stake my claim on the queen. The mating urge tore through me. I came so hard I almost passed out, my come spurting so deeply into her that if she was fertile at all, I couldn't imagine her not getting pregnant. Dread tightened my throat, because we weren't ready for an Isador heir. She wasn't ready. We didn't have a nest. It wasn't safe...

But my body couldn't deny the urge to mate with my bleeding queen.

Panting, I lay on top of her, trying to regain my senses. I couldn't believe I'd come so hard, so quickly. I had no idea if she'd climaxed or not. Until I felt her pleasure humming through the bond like warm, sweet honey. She bit my shoulder, still digging her teeth into the thick muscle, but no fangs. I tore open my wrist and she released the bite to grab my forearm and plant her mouth over the shredded skin. Blood smeared on her lips, her cheeks. Blood dripped on the dress. Splattered crimson on the shining silver. I had to still be fucking high on royal blood to feel like crying at how beautiful she was with my blood on her.

"All clear," Daire said, his voice ringing with intensity.

His polite request to fucking get off our queen and take his position as guard at the door, so he could take my place and feed.

But Shara wasn't ready to let me go. Her eyes gleamed like faceted obsidian, her hunger still strong in the bond. Maybe she needed more blood than usual, since she was losing her own. I rolled off to the side and made room for Daire to take my place.

"Guard?" he growled out, though he was already on the bed and crawling toward her on all fours, very much a prowling warcat.

I felt her search in her mind, reaching out into the night. The thralls were closer, yes, but nothing near enough to threaten the property. Yet.

"Go," I told him.

He paused at her knees and bent his head to lap at the blood on her thighs. Her breath caught and I felt a surge of discomfort from her. Disgust. Periods were a shameful thing in human society. Something to hide. Something gross that no man would want to touch or deal with. Let alone taste.

"We're not men," I reminded her, angry that I hadn't thought to taste that blood myself. "We're Blood. We're Aima. And if you have blood, we want it, like a druggie wants his next hit."

"We live for your blood." Daire licked his lips and came up over her, his breath sighing as she welcomed him inside. Surprisingly, he had more control than me. He wasn't falling on her like a raving lunatic. He even had enough senses remaining to wink at me, though his words were strained. "I'm not the alpha, Rik. I wouldn't mate with her anyway."

She let go of my wrist, and somehow managed to roll Daire off to the side, so she was on top of him. His eyes widened, as surprised as I was. "You're getting stronger too. Not just in power, but physical strength too."

"Good," she panted, throwing her head back so she could rock against him. Her hair trailed down over his thighs, her fingers digging into his chest. "Make him bleed for me."

At her words, his hips arched up off the mattress and tendons stood out on his neck from the force of his thrusts up into her body. I sank my fangs into his throat, taking a taste of him just because I could. His warcat surged in our bond and I could almost smell his fur, feel it soft and warm against my cheek rather than his skin. I leaned back, watching the blood surge up from the punctures. I'd made sure to hit a big vein. My queen wanted blood—she'd get it.

She locked her lips over the wound and made a guttural sound that hit me like a sucker punch. She smeared her hands in his blood, coating his chest, ruining her dress.

And I'd never been so turned on in my life.

I wanted her to finger paint in my blood. Wear us like a second skin. I could see her striding into battle, hair loose and clothed only in our blood.

My dick was already hard again. I wouldn't ever get enough of her. Her taste, her blood, her passion.

I pulled my dick through my hand, rubbing her blood into my flesh. Then I licked my fingers, refusing to waste a single drop.

Shara Isador always tasted like magic. But this…

Fucking off-the-charts goddess level magic that would have leveled me to the ground if I wasn't already on the bed.

Climax roared through me again, taking them both with me. Pleasure richoted in our bond, rippling back and forth, growing exponentially. My pleasure made hers higher; hers sent mine skyrocketing; Daire purred and rumbled and sent us both spiraling again.

I don't know how long we triggered each other, over and over again, but I finally became aware of my surroundings. At some point, I'd transformed into the rock troll, and fuck, he, I, was bigger than ever. Even on my knees beside the bed, my head almost touched the ceiling. I'd have to duck in half to get out of the house. Daire's warcat lay curled around our queen protectively, his sinewy body entwined with hers. His giant head rested on her back, his tail swishing back and forth, golden eyes gleaming in the murk of the room.

Fuck. Darkness had fallen.

Shara lifted her head and swiped her heavy hair out of her

face. Blood smeared her face and throat. Hers, mine, Daire's. He licked the punctures he'd made in her shoulder, making sure they were closed. She looked down at herself, stunned by the gore and stains on the dress. "I've ruined it. How much did this ridiculous dress cost again?"

"It's not ruined." I tried to whisper but the floor boards vibrated with the bass of my troll's voice. "You can call the blood back to you and clean it."

"But it's torn too. I must have gotten tangled up in Daire's claws."

Regret surged through our bond, and shame. That I would not allow. I picked her up as carefully as if she was a butterfly and I'd damage her delicate wings. She wrapped her little arms around my neck without fear, and I wanted to shout to the heavens all the praises to Isis for creating such a queen, and allowing me to be her Blood.

"You can buy a thousand dresses and not put a dent in your legacy."

"I know," she whispered. "But it still feels… wrong. Wasteful. I should have taken it off."

:I for one loved ravaging you in the fairy dress,: Daire's words twined through our bond, rubbing fur deep inside me. *:Keep it on, my queen. Let Greyson in particular see how well we feed you. And how you feed us.:*

Her phone rang. She let go of my neck and I set her down gently so she could rummage through our clothes and find it. "Hello, Dr. Borcht?"

She put the phone on speaker so we could all hear. "Your Majesty, I have your results." Even to my rock troll, the doctor sounded particularly grim.

Shara looked at me, her face paling. "And?"

"I don't know how to tell you this, so I'm just going to give you all the facts."

"Okay."

"You're not half-human, Your Majesty."

Her mouth fell open. "What?"

"You're not half-human. There's no way that Alan Dalton could be your biological father."

Shara sat down on the edge of the bed. "Oh." She swallowed hard, her eyes filling with tears. "He died to keep me safe. He put me on his shoulders to get me away from the monsters. And he wasn't even my father? Then who is?"

"There's no way for me to know at this point, other than to say that part of your DNA is Aima, and the other part is... not. At least not exactly. And not human, either. I have suspicions, but... it's complicated."

"Do you need to run more tests?"

"No," she sighed. "Not unless you want me to test specific DNA to compare to yours to identify and rule out anyone in particular. I meant it's complicated by what I can and cannot say."

"Court politics." She looked up at me, her eyes hardening. "You mean it's something you can't tell me."

"I have suspicions," she repeated. "No proof though. I can only state the facts. You are not half human. And you are not pregnant currently."

"So she's not in heat?" I said.

"I didn't say that," Dr. Borcht replied. "She's not pregnant from the blood I tested from this afternoon. Whether she's ovulating at this time, I can't say. There are some very... interesting... elements in her blood. I have no way of knowing what it all means but I can speculate."

"Tell me," Shara's voice rang, tight with rage and helplessness and yes, grief. It was like she'd lost her father all over again. She's mourned for the human who'd helped raise her... and now had learned there was someone else to mourn. A father she'd never known. "At least what you can."

"Very powerful." Each word was rough, strangled, as though Dr. Borcht had to fight to get them out. "Feared. Too powerful.

Enemies. Your mother—" She gasped, as if in pain. "Not." She cried out and Shara clutched the phone.

"Dr. Borcht? Are you all right?"

Silence on the other end. Then a click. The line went dead.

Shara leaped to her feet. She ended the call and immediately dialed back. The call rolled directly to voice mail.

"Call Gina," I told her, but I feared it was too late. Someone had silenced Dr. Borcht. Hopefully not permanently.

Someone didn't want Shara to know the truth about her parentage.

"Gina, can you check on Dr. Borcht?" Shara paced back and forth at the foot of the bed. "I was talking to her, and the line went dead."

"I'm here at the lab. Hold on. Mala? Are you all right?"

"Yes." At Dr. Borcht's voice, Shara closed her eyes, her shoulders relaxing. She paused the frantic steps.

"Shara was worried about you," Gina said.

"Your Majesty," Dr. Borcht said, taking the phone. "I'm so sorry you were worried. I was..." Her voice thinned, her breathing labored. "Overcome."

That could mean a lot of different things. Overcome by someone? Or overcome by a geas? A spell? An illness?

"Can you tell me anything else?" Shara asked softly.

"Regrettably, I'm afraid not, Your Majesty. Not..." Dr. Borcht sucked in a loud breath. "Now. Another. Time. You..." She cleared her throat forcefully. "You're very strong. I have a feeling that you will be able to take care of this if you set your mind to it."

Something crashed outside and we all jumped. It sounded like a tank was trying to tear down the gate.

I flexed my hands, eager to tear some thralls limb from limb for scaring my queen. Daire leaped down off the bed, claws ticking on the wood floors. "They're here," I said for Dr. Borcht and Gina.

"I can send some private security over to help," Gina said.

"They're human, but trained soldiers. They won't hesitate in shooting something they can't explain and can be trusted not to spread stories about it."

"No," I replied, "but thank you. Our queen has Blood. We will defend her."

Shara ended the call. I could still feel her fear shimmering in the bond, but she tipped her chin up and shook her hair back over her shoulders. "You're not going to lock me up in the basement and leave me while you go fight."

I inclined my head, even though I would have loved to do exactly that. One did not try to keep a queen from the battlefield, though. No matter how much I wanted to keep her safe. "As you wish, Your Majesty."

"How can I fight them?"

:She can use my ketars,: Daire said through the bond.

I dug around in the pile of clothes and found his weapons. I showed her how to wear them, slipping the greaves onto her forearms. The inside grip was made for Daire, and her hands were much smaller. I'd need to make her a custom set of her own if she liked them.

"I do," she whispered, one side of her lips quirking. "You made these? Then I like them even better."

:We joke that he was born in the wrong century because he's a natural blacksmith.:

I watched her give a few experimental swipes. The blades on the ends were wicked sharp. She ought to be able to decapitate anything that came within arms reach, but I didn't intend to let anything get that close to her. "Remember your power, my queen. Leave the physical fighting to us, but use your magic to hurt them."

"What magic? I don't know how to use it."

I picked her up and headed downstairs to see what they'd used to try and breach our defenses.

:You will,: Daire purred through the bond. *:Magic has a way of knowing how to work itself out when your need is great enough.:*

145

19

SHARA

Everything was happening too fast. Just days ago—had it really only been three?— I'd been going about my job as usual, dreading having to move. Now I had two lovers, learned that I was a vampire gazillionaire, and that Dad wasn't my biological father at all. I needed time to process everything, which I didn't have, because monsters were trying to break down the fence protecting the house.

The backyard was completely dark, so it took me a moment to figure out what had taken out the super-bright light pole. A car had crashed into the pole, which now lay over the top of our wrought-iron fence. The fence still stood—but thralls were clambering up the pole, using it as a bridge to get into the yard.

Like a black shadow, Daire silently raced across the yard. As soon as the first monster dropped off the pole inside the fence, he snagged it in his mighty jaws and ripped it in half.

Alrik lumbered over and picked up the pole like it was a toothpick and heaved it back over the fence, shaking monsters off for Daire.

I mostly stood there and felt useless.

Which pissed me off. I had blood simmering in me. Blood

that was supposed to give me powers directly from a goddess. The fuck I was going to stand here and wait for my men to save the day.

But I really had no idea what to do, or how to do it. It was so dark that I couldn't see beyond the fence, so I had no idea how many more monsters were coming, unless I used the mind tapestry. Only I'd have to close my eyes to see the pockets of evil moving toward us, and I didn't want to lose sight of the battle.

I needed some light.

With that thought, I noticed a gleaming ember on my arm. Glowing like a red firefly, the drop of blood spun soft light across my skin. I concentrated on that ember and pictured the other smears and droplets on my body and dress also shining. I would glow like a bonfire. The blood would light up the night. Brighter. I looked back toward the yard and I could see the crashed car now, still smoking. I had no idea monsters could drive cars. That brought a whole new thing to be terrified of.

The ketars Daire had lent to me were too heavy and my hands ached already from holding on to them. Besides, they weren't going to let any of those monsters get anywhere near me. I knew that much. Sighing, I bent down and let go of the handles, leaving them stacked on the ground by the back door.

Blood-red light rose from my skin, flickering like flames. No, the blood really did look like fire. It didn't burn me, though. I touched one of the burning flames and it leaped into my hand, hovering in my palm like a flaming fireball.

Now that was something I could definitely use.

Grinning, I scanned the yard, looking for a monster I could help with. Most of them were still trying to get over the damaged fence, but Daire was easily crunching them into a mass of broken bones and tossing them into a heap on the other side of the fence. Alrik hung back, making sure to grab any that managed to escape the warcat's jaws. He used his fists and simply slammed them into a bloody smear on the snowy ground. I scanned the bushes along the fence, and finally found a monster trying to slide between the narrow iron bars. I didn't think I'd be able to throw it that far though.

Then I gave myself a mental shake. This had nothing to do with my physical prowess, but magic. I didn't have to heave a flaming fireball over a hundred yards. I had to *will* it to hit my target.

I focused on the thrall and envisioned the fireball hitting it. Melting over its skeletal head like candle wax. Lighting its pasty dead skin on fire.

And it worked. The monster burst into flame and let out a glass-shattering shriek. It ran toward the remaining cluster of thralls and I focused on the fire, willing it to spread. One by one they caught fire too and scattered into the night.

Alrik turned toward me and inclined his massive head. "Well done, my queen."

Exhilaration roared through me. I'd been so scared of the monsters all my life. I'd run from town to town, terrified every single night, locked up in four walls, shivering alone, curled up in a fetal position hoping the monsters wouldn't find me one more night. Even when I had to take a stand and fight my way out, I'd been terrified. I'd almost died countless times. A club with a few nails was nothing compared to the ability to light them on fire with a bit of blood.

"Well done," someone said mockingly. "My queen." The last was said with a sneer that I could hear in the words.

Alrik and Daire both closed to me quickly, taking position before me. I don't know how, exactly, but I recognized that voice. Maybe he'd been whispering to me in nightmares my entire life. "Greyson."

"Very good, Shara."

I stepped up between my men so I could search the darkness. His voice was close, but I didn't know where he was. "Why are you trying to kill me?"

"I've never tried to kill you, my queen."

A vicious growl trickled out of Alrik's lips and Daire

148

crouched, ready to pounce. They didn't like anyone calling me that—but them.

"You killed my mother."

"An unfortunate accident. You may not believe me, but I regret any pain I gave her immensely. It was never my intention to kill Selena."

"Come out so we can talk. I want to see you."

Alrik touched my elbow, a slight warning. I had no intention of getting too close, but I needed to put an end to this. Greyson wasn't going to haunt me any longer.

"Oh, I think not." He chuckled, his voice coming from everywhere. Nowhere. "Not yet. Your Blood would not like that much, I'm afraid."

"What do you want, then? Why are you here? Why have you and your monsters hunted me all these years if you didn't want to kill me?"

"Do you know the truth yet, dear, sweet, naive Shara?"

I took a step closer to the fence, but Daire bumped my thigh with his head. *:It's not safe. Don't trust him.:*

:I don't. He's a killer. But he might know who my father is.:

I felt their reluctance in the bond, their alarm and worry ringing like drawn swords in my mind. But I stepped closer to the fence, both of them pressed against me. "What truth?"

Greyson chuckled and I winced, the sharpness in his mirth like metal claws dragging down a chalkboard. "Oh, no, you won't get the secrets from me so easily."

I took another step, almost close enough to touch the iron bars. Daire pressed heavily against my legs, almost tripping me. He didn't want me to get close enough for Greyson or one of the braver thralls to reach through the bars and grab me. Alrik moved behind me and gently drew me back against him so that every inch of my back was safe against his rock-hard bulk. Nothing was going to get to me from the rear. Nothing would get through Daire before me, either.

"Before my Blood came, what would your monsters have done to me if they were able to catch me?"

Greyson made a low, sinister hum that managed to make me shudder despite its soft tones. "They were to bring you to me. Unharmed. Mostly. Though with thralls, you never can tell how well they'll obey when the Master isn't there to force that obedience. They might have had a few tastes of sweet royal blood before I managed to fetch you."

My skin crawled at the thought. "Like you tried to feed from Mom?"

He hissed with a clank of vicious teeth. "Her blood was always mine, and mine was always hers. She learned the truth of that lesson but then it was too late."

"You said you didn't mean to kill her."

"I was her Blood. She was my queen. Even though she left the nest and abandoned us, I was still her Blood. Do you know what that did to me? Do you? Imagine the furry pussy cat, here, still craving your blood. Bound to only you. Hungering for you. Unable to feed on anyone but you. But you change your mind and leave. You cut him off. You turn your back on your power and your legacy and everyone who's sacrificed their entire lives to be at your side. What are they supposed to do then, Shara? Hmm? How are they supposed to live when the very air they breathe is intolerable without your presence?"

I sensed his location near the base of the broken light pole, though I didn't see any movement. Just a feeling of… emptiness. A negative space that tried to say *"nothing to see here."*

"She still loved me," he whispered, and despite everything he'd done, those broken words moved me. Until he continued. "At first, she would sneak out to me occasionally, when the need became too great. We could no longer share power, and watching her wither was the greatest punishment I've ever endured until her death. All because of you, dear Shara. She withered away to nothing for you, and you weren't even hers."

My mind knew that. It was the only logical assumption given

what I'd learned about Aima and the way they conceived. A human man, no matter how much she loved him, couldn't have been her alpha. And if she'd been a breeding queen, she would have pulled Blood to her need. Her alpha—surely Greyson, by the way he'd followed her all these years when none of the other Blood had—would have been driven to mate with her. I would have been his child. Certainly not Dad's.

I wasn't half human and not exactly full Aima either.

So I couldn't be Selena's child.

"Who?" I whispered, my heart breaking all over again. I remembered the night I'd gone to the goddess's pyramid. Mom had said she'd loved me. I knew that. But she'd lied to me my entire life. She'd died to protect me, and I wasn't even hers.

"You know who," Greyson whispered back, cackling beneath his breath. "The nameless one."

My aunt, or rather, Selena's sister. "What did she do to have her name erased like that?"

"She had you."

20

SHARA

My head ached so badly I honestly thought my skull was going to crack open. It felt like one of the ketars was jammed in my left temple. I reached up, touching my head, but it felt normal. No lump, no blood, just pain. Blinding pain that made my knees buckle.

Alrik caught me against him, lifting me up in his arms. "What have you done to her?" he roared.

"Nothing, nothing at all."

I forced my head to turn and I saw him, finally, as he stepped out of the shadows. "Think you the ones who wiped out house Isador will be thrilled to know all their efforts to prevent an heir have failed? Let alone this particular heir. They're very afraid of you, sweetheart. And they should be. Oh yes. We should all be afraid of what Isis has wrought in you."

Despite the ice pick digging into my skull and stirring up my brains, I asked again, "What do you want?"

He came closer, wrapping one pale, dead hand around the iron bar of the gate. He sucked in a breath, a soft hiss of pain, but he didn't release it. "I want to be Blood again."

I blinked rapidly, trying to make my brain work through the

pain. He wanted to be Blood. To a queen. Me. Which meant taking my blood.

:No!: Daire roared in our bond, at the same time that Alrik retorted aloud, "Never."

"Since when does a Blood dictate what his queen can do? Which Blood she can take? When her others come, and they will, my friend, will you tell her no, never, then, too?"

"That's different."

"Is it?" Greyson whispered. "Even if he's a king?"

Alrik trembled, his hands clutching me so hard I couldn't help but gasp with pain. No one had ever said anything about a king. Only Blood and queens. I had no idea what a king was, but by my Blood's reaction, I could only assume it wasn't something he'd be pleased about. But I refused to show my ignorance in front of our enemy.

"Put me down," I said. My voice was weak, shaking from the headache, but Alrik complied immediately. "Daire, move aside."

He did, but when I took another step closer to Greyson, they both stiffened. Our bond blazed with urgency, as if they could hold me back with the force of the blood we'd shared.

Greyson was right... and very wrong at the same time. They did not dictate to me. Even though they were sworn to protect me.

I'd been alone for so long. Scared for so long. Having them with me was great. Fantastic. To be able to sleep, without worrying that something would break through the walls or salt lines to get me. Not to have to run at dawn, every day, hoping and praying I could get away before they tracked me down. I was tired of running.

And yes, I loved the sex. The companionship. The intimacy. I couldn't imagine being alone now.

But if either of them thought that meant I'd be happy sitting back and let others make decisions for me, they were sorely mistaken.

I stepped close enough to lay my hand on top of Greyson's. My fingers instantly went numb, as if he was sucking my essence through that simple contact. But I didn't flinch away or show any emotion on my face. Up close, I could see that he used to be a very handsome man, though years of feeding off humans rather than his queen had damaged his appearance. His skin had grayed, sagged, and drawn back tight across his cheeks, making him look like a corpse. His long silver hair was pulled back in a queue at his neck and he had very aristocratic features. Honestly, he looked more like the traditional vampire prince Vlad than either of my Blood. He even wore an old fashioned suit.

"Are you under the same geas that prevents her name from being spoken?"

"The geas affects only the living, so no," he whispered. "My queen."

Alrik made a sound like a boulder slowly getting crushed into sand, but he didn't interfere.

"Tell me my mother's name, and I'll reward you. I'll give you what you seek."

"Esetta Isador, high queen of Isis."

"And my father?"

"That was not what you offered, my queen."

I inclined my head slightly and allowed a smile to flicker on my lips. "But if you know… Would you tell me?" He hesitated, and I knew I had him. "You loved Selena. You watched over her, didn't you? You only wanted to be with her. I can give you that again."

"Leviathan," he whispered roughly, as if each syllable was pulled roughly from his throat by force.

I felt a dead silence in the bond, a icy shock that made my stomach clench with dread. At least they knew that name, so I'd find out why my parentage was such an issue for the Aima court.

"Thank you." I turned my wrist over, leaving the back of my

hand against his fingers on the fence. "You may have your reward."

He opened his mouth and it took all my will not to flinch back. Long, vicious black teeth tore into my arm. He didn't have a pair of fangs, but a whole mouthful of teeth like a crocodile. I clenched my lips, refusing to cry out. Blood ran down my forearm in thick warm ribbons and puddled on the ground. He threw his head back, my blood dark on his ghastly pale lips. He paused like that, as if waiting for some great miracle. Only nothing changed. He still looked dead. He still had monster teeth and a skeletal face and he certainly didn't gleam and glow with power.

He turned accusing eyes on me. "Give me my power. You promised."

"No." I jerked my hand out of his grip. "I said you would have your reward. What do you think is a fitting reward for the man who killed the only two people who ever loved me?"

He flung himself at the gate, howling, reaching for me through the bars. I didn't step back. I didn't flinch. Instead, I envisioned every drop of my blood inside him catching fire.

His eyes flared wide. He clawed at his face, tearing open the paper white skin. He opened his mouth to scream and flames blasted up his throat. His suit caught fire. He fell to the ground, screaming, howling, tearing at himself as if he could release my blood before I managed to kill him.

Because that's exactly what I intended to do.

21

ALRIK

I learned some very important truths about my queen this evening.

Her first gift from Isis was fire. And Shara Isador was not to be fucked with.

Greyson learned that lesson too as he burst into flame. She stood there, bleeding, until he was only a smear in the snow.

Softly, she asked, "Is he dead? Really dead?"

Daire leaped over the fence and batted one big paw at the stinking heap of ash. *:Most definitely.:*

"Good." She turned to face me and swayed slightly. I caught her as her knees gave way. "Then he got what he wanted most of all."

I carried her inside and up to her bed. I didn't think the blood loss was affecting her, though she had definitely lost a large amount tonight, between us feeding from her and her ordeal with the thrall. No, she suffered from shock. Mental shock. Through our bond, I could feel the fragile tenderness in her temple where the pain had struck. Someone had intended her harm, or at least tried to stop her from learning anything about her parentage. One of Triune? A queen who wanted the third seat? Who had silenced Dr. Borcht? There was no way to know for certain, at least not yet.

I lay her gently on the bed and transformed back so I could hold her without worrying I might kill her if I sneezed. Daire lapped at her wrist, gently cleaning the jagged skin. Greyson had torn her wrist severely. She'd need a large quantity of blood from us to ensure it healed overnight.

Far from a hardship.

I stretched out beside her and drew her face to my throat. She nuzzled me, but didn't try to bite. "Who's Leviathan?"

Daire transformed too, joining us on the bed so we could hold her between us. "Not a who, but what."

She stared to lift her head, to turn and look at him, so I answered quickly to keep her close. "Leviathan is a…" I hesitated, not wanting to worry her. She sent a hint of fire flooding through our bond, and I couldn't help but remember the way the thralls had crisped. Though I knew she wouldn't do that to me. At least deliberately. "Well, you would call him a demon."

"A great demonic dragon," Daire added, not so helpfully. "I think he's even mentioned in the Bible."

"So I'm not half-human… but half-demon?" Her voice rose. "Is that possible?"

"Anything is possible."

"Demons are evil. They're from hell. Right?"

"Triune courts are complicated, and can certainly be compared to hell." I tucked her tighter against me, as if that alone would protect her. "Demons are closer to Aima than human, and we all come from Gaia. Some simply took a darker path and ended as part of the Skotos court, rather than the Aima court. They're still Triune."

"What if he's right? What if my father was a… a… dragon demon?"

Giving up on feeding her, at least for the moment, I tipped her chin up so I could look her in the eyes. "You're my queen.

I'm your Blood. I don't give a fuck who your parents are. Nothing has changed between this Blood and his queen."

Her eyes filled with tears and overflowed, shaking me to my core. I clutched her harder against me, smoothing her hair frantically. "Please don't cry, my queen. All will be well. I swear it. We will find out the truth of things for you."

Daire rested his chin on her shoulder. "I should go piss on that pile of charred bones for upsetting you."

She made a sound, ragged, harsh, and I glared at him. Until I realized that was laughter, not more tears. "Thank you, my Blood."

I searched her eyes and wiped her tears away. "For what?"

"For wanting me to stay your queen even if I'm half demon."

"I want you." My voice rumbled deeper bass, but I didn't try to lighten my tone. I wanted her to hear and know the truth of my words. "I love you. You're my life, Shara."

"Don't say that," she whispered, reaching up to cup my cheek. I turned my face into her palm, rubbing on her hand. "If something happens to me, I don't want you to end up like Greyson."

I looked at Daire over her shoulder. We didn't need the Blood bond to agree. I looked back into her eyes and gripped her chin, firmly enough her eyes narrowed a little, her pride bristling. "For one thing, if something happens to you, that means Daire and I are both already dead, happily, because that means we died protecting you. But if goddess forbid something did take you from us, we will follow you in death. We will kill each other before either of us roams the earth like him."

Her eyes softened. "Let's hope nothing happens to any of us."

"Agreed," Daire said. "And can we also agree that you should tear into Rik and drink your fill from him before you rest?"

"Definitely." I released her chin and offered my throat. But she only stared at me, her eyes going dark and sad again. "What's wrong?"

"What if I never get fangs? What if I can't ever feed from you without some assistance?"

Daire leaned up and bit me so hard I growled at him. The fucking asshole had torn a chunk out of my throat.

"Then it's my great pleasure to offer my assistance, my queen."

22

SHARA

I walked across moonlit sands toward the golden pyramid. Wind glided over the dunes, a soft whisper of night's secrets, lightly perfumed with jasmine. Mom stood at the pyramid, staring at me. She moved her mouth, and though I couldn't hear her words, I knew what she said. *"I'm so sorry. I always loved you. So did she."*

She. My birth mother, whose name no one living was allowed to utter.

A man ran across the dunes, effortlessly floating across the shifting sands. Long silver hair fell loose about Greyson's shoulders, his coat flapping about him like wings. Or maybe that was wings. It was hard to tell. He ran straight to Mom and fell to his knees in front of her. She wrapped her arms around him and pulled his head against her breasts. Their love radiated like a soft glow into the night.

She looked at me, her eyes streaming with tears. *"Thank you."*

There were so many things I wanted to ask her, but I wasn't sure that I wanted the answers. Or that she'd be allowed to tell me, even if she was willing. Had she really loved Dad enough to leave her nest and give up her power? Had she regretted giving up Greyson? Had she really gone to him off and on for years after leaving court?

Had she ever regretted taking me in, raising me as her own?

Before I could ask and shatter the pleasant memories I had of her as my mother, I turned away and walked into the night. The pyramid wasn't for me tonight. I didn't feel drawn there.

Suddenly I was in my backyard in Kansas City. Roses bloomed along the fence and the air felt warm and thick like a hot July night. I looked up at the house, and didn't feel a sense of home or gladness. Even though light spilled through the colored glass window above the front entry, the one I'd loved so much as a child. I didn't feel drawn here. I didn't want to stay. Nothing held me here but memories.

I would find my own place of safety. I would build my own nest.

I closed my eyes and tipped my head back, letting the moon-light shine on my face. Spreading my arms, I cast my will out into the night, feeling, seeking anything of interest. I glided through the night on silent wings like a great bird of prey. Something pinged, drawing me south. I looked down at the city nestled in the cliffs and hills and recognized Eureka Springs. I had felt a deep resonance there, as if some part of my heart recognized it, though I'd never been there before.

I landed and walked on bare feet through the woods. Pine needles and snow muffled my steps. The trees parted and a magnificent river stretched out before me, shining in the moon-light like polished silver and frosted glass. Rocky cliffs rose across the water and on top of the steep drop off, a large house sprawled in the trees. Odd medieval-looking towers, many roofs, a jumble of buildings that didn't really seem to go together. But to me, that was its charm. I took a mental snapshot of the place so I could describe it to Gina. I wanted to find this place and make it my own.

Something came through the trees behind me. Twigs snap-ping. Pine boughs dropping clumps of soft snow to the ground.

A heavy click. The ruffle of massive wings. Something brushed my cheek, soft like feathers.

"I will find you here, my queen."

I turned my head, nuzzling my cheek through downy feathers. Black, soft, shiny, even in the moonlight. He smelled like blood and magic. Old magic. But not snakes. I didn't think he was the one I'd dreamed about before. "Who are you, my Blood?"

"Nevarre." His voice rang like drawn steel, his feathers bristling around me. "But I cannot be your Blood, my queen."

His accent sounded British, or maybe Australian. I couldn't tell. "Why not?"

"Because I'm already dead."

I lifted my head, intending to search his face for answers, but he tightened his grip on me and talons pierced my skin.

The scent of my blood spiked my hunger. I suddenly wanted this man's blood.

So I opened my mouth and sank razor teeth into him. Not fangs, but many sharp, pointed teeth. Like Greyson's.

I JERKED awake and sat up, panting. Alrik quickly sat up too, his arm going around me, drawing me close. Intensity vibrated through his muscles and I felt him scanning the room, listening for any threat. "What is it? What's wrong?"

I started to say nothing, but there was something in my mouth. I tasted blood. I spat out the thing in my mouth.

A black feather lay wet on my thigh. Wet with blood.

I shuddered, wiping my mouth. Yes, I still tasted him.

Alrik picked up the feather and smelled it. "A raven." He took another deep breath. "Druid." His concern leaked into me. Not even a vampire would take Druid magic lightly. "Did he say anything to you?"

I pressed against him, wrapping my arms around his waist.

Breathing in his comforting scent, soaking in his strength. "He said he would find me in Eureka Springs."

His chest rumbled beneath my ear, a soothing sound not unlike Daire's purr. "If you want to find him, then that's where we'll go. If you don't..."

"My nest will be there. I saw it."

He lay back, drawing me onto his chest so every inch of me pressed against him. His big hands stroked up and down my back, soothing me. "Then he must be Blood. That's a good thing."

I lifted my head so I could see his face. "But he said he couldn't be Blood because he was already dead."

Alrik's eyes flared a moment, then narrowed. "Did he give a name?"

"Nevarre." I could see the connections flaring through his mind, lightning fast. A raven with Druid magic. Seeking me at my future nest. "Could he be the king that Greyson mentioned? What is a king anyway?"

"Queens are rare among our kind, a blessing from the old goddesses, but a king is only born once every thousand years or more, and usually killed at birth or at least exiled. They're not a blessing, but an aberration."

Babies, killed or exiled? That seemed extremely drastic. "Why?"

"Kings are born with power of their own. They don't need or even want a queen, which makes them extremely volatile. Honestly, they're usually driven mad before they reach adulthood, overcome with powers they can't control, urges they don't understand, and no one can help them tame those dark needs. As a young male, I heard the tales of Aima kings gone mad, ravaging entire nests, killing his queen mother and any other heirs. Slaughtering Blood as easily as humans. These stories were our form of the Boogie Man, I guess. Even the Skotos Triune will exile a king to protect their queens."

"The raven didn't seem crazy, just... angry. Angry that he was too late. Do you have any idea who he could be?"

"A raven with Druid magic would very likely be from the Morrigan's house."

I didn't know a lot about ancient goddesses, but even I knew that another name for the Morrigan was the Phantom Queen. I buried my face against his throat and a heavy pang thudded my heart. "I bit him, but I didn't have fangs. It was awful. I had teeth like Greyson."

Unbothered by my admission, Alrik kissed the top of my head and squeezed me gently. "I won't mind whatever teeth you have."

He might not mind crocodile teeth on his queen, but I felt his unease through the bond. He wanted me safe. That meant more Blood. But he wanted to remain as my alpha, too.

If a king was meant to join me...

Did a king overtake the alpha's position? I was afraid to ask, but his worry told me that his position would very likely be at risk.

Which I didn't like. Not one bit. I wanted him and Daire like this. Every night. I couldn't imagine anyone else inserting himself between us.

I felt Daire before I heard him. In his warcat form, he padded into the room and jumped onto the bed beside me. I rolled over and rubbed my face into his fur and he rumbled out a deep, bone-rattling purr.

:I believe someone approaches, my queen.:

My heart pounded and ice trickled down my spine. But Alrik only folded tighter against my back, pressing me against Daire. "He said *someone*, not a threat."

Daire shifted to his human form, letting me feel his fur melt away to hot muscled flesh. "I feel someone out there, but I couldn't get a good scent yet. I'm guessing he'll arrive midday."

I closed my eyes, relaxing back into their arms. I pulled up the tapestry of our surroundings and immediately, my attention was drawn to the east by a red glow, like a campfire burned in the wilderness. I touched the glow, soaking in as much as I could despite the distance separating us. Male. Older, scarred, tough. At my touch, he flared brighter and I had a sense of galloping hooves. "That's what you looked like when I first felt you."

"Then a third Blood will soon join our ranks." Through our bond, I felt Alrik stretch toward that red glow. He prodded, hard, and the glow flickered and warmed, but it didn't go out or blaze taller. Just hotter. He blew out a breath and seemed satisfied with whatever he'd found.

I rolled over and looked at him, one brow arched. "What was that about?"

Daire chuckled. "It's the Bloods' way of seeing whose dick is bigger. Our big guy won, by the way. Rik is still alpha."

"As if there was any doubt." He flashed a grin at my words and nudged me with his bigger dick. Daire kissed my nape, his still very impressive dick like a hot rod against my ass. Desire flooded me, my core already aching. In the night, I felt that red glow burn hotter. The campfire burst into wildfire as he thundered toward us. "We're definitely going to need a bigger bed."

BE sure to sign up for Joely's newsletter to find out when the follow-up, QUEEN TAKES KING, is available! Keep reading for a preview.

PREVIEW OF QUEEN TAKES KING

SHARA

Two gorgeous men asleep in my bed.

Merry fucking Christmas to me.

I stretched and felt a dull ache between my legs, and no wonder. I certainly wasn't used to having sex. Let alone with two men who were completely dedicated to blowing my mind as often as possible.

I could do without the miserable cramps though. It was so unfair that I was a vampire, but still had to deal with a period that came like clockwork.

I stared up at the ceiling, running through everything I'd learned.

Just four days ago, my life had turned upside down. I still couldn't believe it.

Mom was actually my aunt and the man I'd called Dad wasn't my biological father either.

I wasn't human. I wasn't even half human. But Dr. Borcht didn't know exactly what I was, either.

I had enough Aima blood—directly descended from the goddess, Isis—to be a vampire queen. Hence the two lovers, who called themselves my Blood, sworn to protect and please me, no matter what I ordered. (So they claimed.)

At some point when coming into my power the first time, I'd even died, though being a descendant of the goddess of resurrection had some major advantages.

Last night, I'd killed the man who murdered Mom. I'd burned him to death. With my blood.

It scared me how... okay... I was about that.

I didn't want to end up being a greater monster myself than the ones who'd killed my parents.

I'd never killed anything before, except the occasional spider. Greyson Isador was a murderer. He was directly responsible for both of my parents' deaths, and countless other humans he'd turned into his thralls, the gray lifeless demon-creatures who'd hunted me my entire life.

He deserved to die.

That didn't make me feel better. Because I was still glad he was dead. And I was glad I'd been the one to finish him.

What else would I end up being glad about?

I had no idea what time it was, but I didn't think I'd be able to fall back asleep. I tried to get up carefully without waking up the guys, but I lifted my head and Alrik's popped open.

As my alpha Blood, he was the biggest, baddest man I'd ever seen. He looked like he'd walked off a superhero movie set.

"My queen?" He whispered, but my other Blood lifted his head too.

"Sorry, I didn't mean to wake you."

"We live to serve." Daire stretched as only a cat can do, like every muscle in his body had a kink in it. "Even if it's fucking six o'clock in the morning."

"It is? How do you know?"

He rolled over and faced me, smiling so his dimple showed in his cheek. "I have no idea what time it is. It just feels early. Are you well?"

"No," Alrik said before I could, a frown grooving his fore-head. "You hurt. Is this normal when you menstruate?"

"Unfortunately, yes. Though that's a human thing. I have no idea why I'm so lucky to have cramps like this when I'm not even human."

I sat up, trying to think of a graceful way to escape to the bathroom when I'm sure I was bleeding heavily. "I really should have put a tampon in last night."

Alrik made a low, rumbly noise that was somewhere between the growl of a distant storm and the thunderous purr of some great beast. "There's no need, my queen. If you lie back, I'll be more than happy to clean you up."

Ew. Gross. It made me cringe. Human sensibilities, I guess.

Daire cocked an eyebrow at me. "It's our nature. Even more so for Rik. He'll be hard pressed to leave you alone for an hour when you smell so…" He inhaled deeply, running his nose along my arm. "Good."

As the alpha Blood, Alrik would evidently be the one to mate with me, if I ever decided to have a child. Aima women only menstruated when they were in heat, ready to breed. The better to attract the male vampire, my sweet. So me bleeding was going to drive the big guy nuts.

He rubbed his face across my shoulder to my back, one big arm coming around my waist. His fingers dipped lower, cupping my pussy, and he shuddered against me.

Power rose in me. The hairs on my arms rose, the charge building in the air around me. Yesterday, I'd tried to tap that power to fix my hair, and about blew the top of my head off. And I'd only been flowing a trickle. This felt like a mess.

A mess to me, maybe, but not to him. He rubbed his hand over me, not stroking me, exactly, but just holding my pussy, treasuring me. Blood and all. Despite my hang ups, my head still fell back against his shoulder and I opened my legs wider. Need rose in me. His mouth pressed against my ear, his breath hot on my skin. His tongue dipped into my ear as his fingers slid deeper. One finger inside me, his thumb rubbing my clit. So slow and languorous, as if he was in no rush. I'd always thought foreplay involved the guy getting the girl off as quickly as possible so he could get on with his own business.

But not Rik. And not Daire either.

I opened my eyes, checking to see where Daire had gone.

"I asked him to start the coffee," Rik whispered against my ear, twisting his finger deeper, making my hips arch into his hand.

"You asked him to leave?"

"Yes. I'm his alpha. He'll do as I tell him. Even when he doesn't want to."

"What if I wanted him here? With us?"

Rik's hand stilled. "With a thought, I'll call him back, my queen. But remember his nature. He won't be able to resist licking what I merely pet."

My stomach trembled, my brain quailed, but my body thought that was a brilliant idea. Through his bond, I could feel his hunger. He wanted to bury his head between my thighs too. More than anything. Need pounded like a jackhammer in his skull. He needed to mate. More, his queen needed him, evidenced by the blood, which to him meant breeding time. It was meant to drive him crazy, and it was.

Yet he only stroked me.

Just feeling his need was almost enough to convince me I should allow him to do as he wished. It would have been really easy for him to kiss and cajole me into going along with his need. In fact, I couldn't believe he wasn't, especially as badly as he felt. His urge to mate was just as urgent as his need to breathe after being submerged in water. He was drowning, driven to the point of madness by his own body's impulses. Yet without the bond, I wouldn't have even known.

"I would like nothing better than to feast on your blood,

from whatever part of your body it came. But you would not enjoy it, and so I will not, either. If there comes a time you'd welcome me in that regard, know that I'm more than eager. Any of us will be. It would be a priceless gift to us. And yes, the power kick from a breeding queen is insane."

I was relieved—but a little disappointed and guilty too. I didn't like denying him when he'd do anything to please me. "But I'm not breeding. It's just my period."

"We don't know that you aren't breeding too. And by your scent…" he rubbed his face up the column of my throat and pressed his nose behind my ear, up under my hair, and breathed deeply. "You're breeding. That's what your scent and your body are telling me. Fuck. Would it upset you if I tasted your blood from my hand?"

Blood itself didn't bother me. It was just the whole period aspect that put a damper on sharing that particular blood. But I'd love to watch him do something that would bring him so much pleasure. I pulled away enough to turn and face him. "You can on one condition. I want you to come when you taste it."

His eyes smoldered, his mouth partly opened, his lips full like he'd been kissing me senseless for days. His fangs had descended too, making a surge of desire crest inside me. I knew the pleasure he could bring with those fangs. His vampire sensibilities knew exactly when to bite to maximize my pleasure. But this time he wouldn't have to bite to taste my blood.

Or to make me come. Because I had a feeling I was going to be able to climax just from watching him.

Reaching over with his clean left hand, he dragged his palm up my slit, hand cupped, catching everything he could get. He wrapped his bloody right hand around his dick and hissed. His nostrils flared, a muscle in his cheek ticking as he restrained himself. But he didn't pump his cock at all. He just smeared my blood over himself, running his hand up over the head and down the sides. His shoulders bunched, his neck corded, and I shuddered at the memory of having him on top of me. Inside me. All that power. All that force. Thrusting into me.

He lifted his left hand up to his mouth, closed his eyes, and tipped his palm, letting my blood slide into his mouth. I felt the rush of fire exploding through his veins. His muscles twitched like a live wire jumped inside him. He let out a guttural cry and arched his back, shaking as he came, hard. Every shudder pushing me closer to the edge as he licked his palm. Sucked his fingers. Making sure to get every drop.

And I couldn't help myself. I threw myself at him and locked my mouth to his throat. I bit him, willing my fangs to emerge. I wanted to have his blood filling my mouth. I wanted to hear him groan with the sweet pain as I penetrated him. I wanted to take him, possess him, as he had done to me.

He cupped my pussy again, sliding his fingers deep inside me, filling me, and climax rumbled through me. I came. But it wasn't what I wanted. At all.

I buried my face against his throat and fought not to cry.

"Let me——"

"No," I retorted, refusing to look up at him. "I don't want you to tear open a vein for me."

"If you hunger——"

"I want to be able to do it myself. Do other queens have this issue? Have you ever heard of a queen with no fangs?"

"You have fangs. You felt them. It's just not… time."

I pulled away, avoiding his gaze, and climbed out of bed. "I'm going to take a shower. A real shower."

"Shara…"

I paused but didn't look back at him. "I won't feed again until I can bite you myself."

"Don't say that." He got up too, coming to my side to wrap his arms around me, but I didn't soften. I didn't yield into his arms. He wanted to comfort me. Placate me. Distract me. "You need blood, now more than ever. You need to be strong."

"I'm Isis's last queen and I can't even take blood myself.

Everyone keeps telling me that the other queens will want me dead, but they'll only laugh when they see what a sorry excuse for a vampire I am. I can't even bite my own Blood to feed myself."

He rested his chin on my head, his arms steady around me. "This Blood in particular will open every vein on his body for you before you can even ask."

Steel hardened inside me. "As Isis is my witness, I won't ask."

ALRIK

I STARED at the bathroom door worriedly. She needed to feed. This was a crucial time in her ascension as the Isador queen. The more blood she took, the more powerful she'd be, and yeah, she was already fucking powerful. But it was raw and untapped. She needed time to hone her magic, and she wouldn't have that time if she wasn't strong enough to keep the other queens away based on sheer strength.

More troubling, though, was her adamancy. The ancient gods loved nothing more than one of their creations making such an oath, which opened the door for the deity to fuck with them. I didn't believe Isis hovered over this house listening to Her last queen's words, but that kind of refusal might have drawn the goddess's attention. And when a goddess wanted Her last queen strong…

She'd answer that prayer, that oath, but not necessarily in a way that Shara would approve.

I went back upstairs to the tower room and stripped the bed linens for her. It would upset her if she came back in and found Daire crouched on the mattress feeding on the soiled spots, and without a doubt, I knew he'd do exactly that. She could have called the blood to her and returned her energy somewhat, but she'd been too upset. Her emotions were volatile, and not just because of her period. Though that certainly didn't help.

Her whole world had changed in the span of a few days, and this was just the tip of the iceberg.

:Rik, you need to see this.: Daire said through our bond, alert, but not alarmed, so I didn't tromp downstairs like we were under attack.

I found him in the living room with the television on the local news station. As soon as I entered, he unpaused the show.

"A clothing store in the Power and Light District was vandalized overnight," the anchorwoman said. "They provided an exclusive to us of the security camera footage. Brace yourself, folks, because this is definitely something in the realm of 'we have no idea what this is.'"

A grainy black-and-white film played on the screen, displaying the front entrance. The glass exploded and two shapes appeared on screen.

I groaned. Thralls. Captured on human surveillance.

The news channel paused the security tape with a thrall prominently frozen on the screen. It was definitely human-shaped, though bent and lanky. Its eyes glowed oddly and teeth glistened.

"Police believe that two people dressed like monsters in order to break into the store. But what we find odd is that the store owner doesn't believe anything was stolen. One dressing room was ransacked but other than the front door, there was no other damage and nothing else was taken. I don't know, Bob. Does that look like two punks dressed up for Halloween—in December, no less—to you?"

The other anchorman, Bob, shuddered. "It sure doesn't, Helen."

We'd had thralls caught on television before. It wasn't ideal, but Shara was right. With modern technology, it was impossible to prevent detection. Most of the time, the human mind dismissed what it couldn't understand. Or came up with some other explanation, like kids dressed up in costumes. That was easier to believe than monsters roaming the countryside. "That's not too bad," I said to Daire, but he shook his head and let the show continue.

"Maybe it's a coincidence," a woman said into a male journalist's microphone. I recognized her as the sales woman who'd helped us yesterday. "But we had an unusual customer yesterday who used that changing room. A very beautiful woman, with two incredible men. They referred to her as queen."

"Queen?" The man asked. "Like 'Your Majesty?'"

"Yes. He called her that. He even went down on his knees at one point. And she spent…" The sales woman's eyes widened, catching herself before blurting out an amount. "A lot. We're supposed to deliver it today."

"The hell you are," I retorted.

"I gave her our address," Daire said.

"Fuck. The last thing we need right now is a bunch of curious reporters spreading tales about a queen in Kansas City."

"We'd better call Gina."

The doorbell rang. Daire checked through the peephole before opening the door to the very person we'd been talking about. She saw the television on and nodded. "Good. You've seen. Has she?"

"Not yet." My first reaction was to send Daire to knock on the door, but that was ridiculous when I had a bond with her. I just hesitated to intrude when she was obviously upset and needed some space, and Daire's lighter personality might be more welcome than mine. *:My queen.:*

:Yes?:

Her emotions felt calmer in the bond. She'd mentioned a bath before too. Evidently the hot water was definitely something I needed to be sure she indulged in when she was upset and stressed out. However, she was still worried she might never be the queen I expected her to be, which was nonsense. I had no expectations other than she take my blood whenever she wanted. I let her feel that shining in the bond, though I didn't say the words. *:We have a situation. Gina's here to discuss.:*

Mentally she sighed. *:I'll be right there.:*

ABOUT THE AUTHOR

Joely Sue Burkhart has always loved heroes who hide behind a mask, the darker and more dangerous the better. Whether cool, sophisticated billionaire, brutal bloodthirsty assassin, or simply a man tortured by his own needs, they all wear masks to protect themselves. Once they finally give you a peek into the passionate, twisted secrets they're hiding, they always fall hard and fast. Dare to look beneath the mask with delicious BDSM in a wide variety of genres with Joely on her website, www.joelysue-burkhart.com.

If you have Kindle Unlimited, you can read all her indie books for free!

Wondering what's next? Sign up for her newsletter and receive exclusive free content.

Free in Kindle Unlimited

BEAUTIFUL DEATH

The Connaghers, contemporary erotic romance

Free in Kindle Unlimited

LETTERS TO AN ENGLISH PROFESSOR

DEAR SIR, I'M YOURS

HURT ME SO GOOD

YOURS TO TAKE

NEVER LET YOU DOWN

MINE TO BREAK

Billionaires in Bondage, contemporary erotic romance

(re-releasing in 2017 from Entangled Publishing)

THE BILLIONAIRE SUBMISSIVE

THE BILLIONAIRE'S INK MISTRESS

THE BILLIONAIRE'S CHRISTMAS BARGAIN

The Wellspring Chronicles, erotic fantasy

Free in Kindle Unlimited

NIGHTGAZER

A Killer Need, Erotic Romantic Suspense

ONE CUT DEEPER

TWO CUTS DARKER

THREE CUTS DEADER

A Jane Austen Space Opera, SF/Steampunk erotic romance

(re-releasing in 2017)

LADY WYRE'S REGRET, free read prequel

LADY DOCTOR WYRE

HER GRACE'S STABLE

LORD REGRET'S PRICE

Historical Fantasy Erotica

GOLDEN

The Maya Bloodgates, paranormal romance

BLOODGATE, free read prequel

THE BLOODGATE GUARDIAN

THE BLOODGATE WARRIOR

Made in United States
Troutdale, OR
03/12/2024

18401110R00106